Edith Nash Volk.

August 31, 1923.

THE GIANT SCISSORS

JULES.

THE GIANT SCISSORS

BY

ANNIE FELLOWS JOHNSTON

AUTHOR OF "THE LITTLE COLONEL,"
"BIG BROTHER," "OLE MAMMY'S
TORMENT," ETC.

Illustrated by
ETHELDRED B. BARRY

BOSTON
THE PAGE COMPANY
PUBLISHERS

Twenty-third Impression, May, 1920

CONTENTS

24444

ILLVSTRATIONS

THE GATE OF THE GIANT SCISSORS.

CHAPTER I.

IN THE PEAR-TREE.

JOYCE was crying, up in old Monsieur Gréville's tallest pear-tree. She had gone down to the farthest corner of the garden, out of sight of the house, for she did not want any one to know that she was miserable enough to cry.

She was tired of the garden with the high stone wall around it, that made her feel like a prisoner; she was tired of French verbs and foreign faces; she was tired of France, and so homesick for her mother and Jack and Holland and the baby, that she couldn't help crying.

No wonder, for she was only twelve years old, and she had never been out of the little Western village where she was born, until the day she started abroad with her Cousin Kate.

Now she sat perched up on a limb in a dismal bunch, her chin in her hands and her elbows on her knees. It was a gray afternoon in November; the air was frosty, although the laurel-bushes in the garden were all in bloom.

"I s'pect there is snow on the ground at home," thought Joyce, "and there's a big, cheerful fire in the sitting-room grate.

"Holland and the baby are shelling corn, and Mary is popping it. Dear me! I can smell it just as plain! Jack will be coming in from the post-office pretty soon, and maybe he'll have one of my letters. Mother will read it out loud, and there they'll all be, thinking that I am having such a fine time; that it is such a grand thing for me to be abroad studying, and having dinner served at night in so many courses, and all that sort of thing. They don't know that I am sitting up here in this pear-tree, lonesome enough to die. Oh, if I could only go back home and see them for even five minutes," she sobbed, "but I can't!

I can't! There's a whole wide ocean between us!"

She shut her eyes, and leaned back against the tree as that desolate feeling of homesickness settled over her like a great miserable ache. Then she found that shutting her eyes, and thinking very hard about the little brown house at home, seemed to bring it into plain sight. It was like opening a book, and seeing picture after picture as she turned the pages.

There they were in the kitchen, washing dishes, she and Mary; and Mary was standing on a soap-box to make her tall enough to handle the dishes easily. How her funny little braid of yellow hair bobbed up and down as she worked, and how her dear little freckled face beamed, as they told stories to each other to make the work seem easier.

Mary's stories all began the same way: "If I had a witch with a wand, this is what we would do." The witch with a wand had come to Joyce in the shape of Cousin Kate Ware, and that coming was one of the pictures that Joyce could see now, as she thought about it with her eyes closed.

There was Holland swinging on the gate,

waiting for her to come home from school, and trying to tell her by excited gestures, long before she was within speaking distance, that some one was in the parlor. The baby had on his best plaid kilt and new tie, and the tired little mother was sitting talking in the parlor. an unusual thing for her. Joyce could see herself going up the path, swinging her sun-bonnet by the strings and taking hurried little bites of a big June apple in order to finish it before going into the house. Now she was sitting on the sofa beside Cousin Kate, feeling very awkward and shy with her little brown fingers clasped in this stranger's soft white hand. She had heard that Cousin Kate was a very rich old maid, who had spent years abroad, studying music and languages, and she had expected to see a stout, homely woman with bushy eyebrows, like Miss Teckla Schaum, who played the church organ, and taught German in the High School.

But Cousin Kate was altogether unlike Miss Teckla. She was tall and slender, she was young-looking and pretty, and there was a stylish air about her, from the waves of her soft golden brown hair to the bottom of her tailor-made gown, that was not often seen in this little Western village.

Joyce saw herself glancing admiringly at Cousin Kate, and then pulling down her dress as far as possible, painfully conscious that her shoes were untied, and white with dust. The next picture was several days later. She and Jack were playing mumble-peg outside under the window by the lilac-bushes, and the little mother was just inside the door, bending over a pile of photographs that Cousin Kate had dropped in her lap. Cousin Kate was saying, "This beautiful old French villa is where I expect to spend the winter, Aunt Emily. These are views of Tours, the town that lies across the river Loire from it, and these are some of the châteaux near by that I intend to visit. They say the purest French in the world is spoken there. I have prevailed on one of the dearest old ladies that ever lived to give me rooms with her. She and her husband live all alone in this big country place, so I shall have to provide against loneliness by taking my company with me. Will you let me have Joyce for a year?"

Jack and she stopped playing in sheer aston

ishment, while Cousin Kate went on to explain how many advantages she could give the little girl to whom she had taken such a strong fancy.

Looking through the lilac-bushes, Joyce could see her mother wipe her eyes and say, "It seems like pure providence, Kate, and I can t stand in the child's way. She'll have to support herself soon, and ought to be prepared for it; but she's the oldest of the five, you know, and she has been like my right hand ever since her father died. There'll not be a minute while she is gone, that I shall not miss her and wish her back. She's the life and sunshine of the whole home."

Then Joyce could see the little brown house turned all topsy-turvy in the whirl of preparation that followed, and the next thing, she was standing on the platform at the station, with her new steamer trunk beside her. Half the town was there to bid her good-by. In the excitement of finding herself a person of such importance she forgot how much she was leaving behind her, until looking up, she saw a tender, wistful smile on her mother's face, sadder than any tears.

Luckily the locomotive whistled just then,

WHERE JOYCE LIVED.

and the novelty of getting aboard a train for
the first time, helped her to be brave at the
parting.   She stood on the rear platform of
the last car, waving her handkerchief to the
group at the station as long as it was in sight,
so that the last glimpse her mother should
have of her, was with her bright little face all
ashine.

All these pictures passed so rapidly through
Joyce's mind, that she had retraced the experiences of the last three months in as many minutes.   Then, somehow, she felt better.   The
tears had washed away the ache in her throat.
She wiped her eyes and climbed liked a squirrel
to the highest limb that could bear her weight.

This was not the first time that the old pear-
tree had been shaken by Joyce's grief, and it
knew that her spells of homesickness always
ended in this way.   There she sat, swinging her
plump legs back and forth, her long light hair
blowing over the shoulders of her blue jacket,
and her saucy little mouth puckered into a soft
whistle.   She could see over the high wall now.
The sun was going down behind the tall Lom-
bardy poplars that lined the road, and in a distant field two peasants still at work reminded

her of the picture of "The Angelus." They seemed like acquaintances on account of the resemblance, for there was a copy of the picture in her little bedroom at home.

All around her stretched quiet fields, sloping down to the ancient village of St. Symphorien and the river Loire. Just across the river, so near that she could hear the ringing of the cathedral bell, lay the famous old town of Tours. There was something in these country sights and sounds that soothed her with their homely cheerfulness. The crowing of a rooster and the barking of a dog fell on her ear like familiar music.

"It's a comfort to hear something speak English," she sighed, "even if it's nothing but a chicken. I do wish that Cousin Kate wouldn't be so particular about my using French all day long. The one little half-hour at bedtime when she allows me to speak English isn't a drop in the bucket. It's a mercy that I had studied French some before I came, or I would have a lonesome time. I wouldn't be able to ever talk at all."

It was getting cold up in the pear-tree. Joyce shivered and stepped down to the limb below, but paused in her descent to watch a peddler going down the road with a pack on his back.

"Oh, he is stopping at the gate with the b i g scissors!" she cried, so interested that she spoke aloud. "I must wait to see if it opens."

There was some-thing m y s t e r i o u s about that gate across the road. Like Monsieur Gréville's, it was plain and solid, reaching as high as the wall. Only the lime-trees and the second story win-

dows of the house could be seen above it. On the top it bore an iron medallion, on which was fastened a huge pair of scissors. There was a smaller pair on each gable of the house, also.

During the three months that Joyce had

been in Monsieur Gréville's home, she had watched every day to see it open; but if any one ever entered or left the place, it was certainly by some other way than this queer gate.

What lay beyond it, no one could tell. She had questioned Gabriel the coachman, and Berthe the maid, in vain. Madame Gréville said that she remembered having heard, when a child, that the man who built it was named *Ciseaux*, and that was why the symbol of this name was hung over the gate and on the gables. He had been regarded as half crazy by his neighbors. The place was still owned by a descendant of his, who had gone to Algiers, and left it in charge of two servants.

The peddler rang the bell of the gate several times, but failing to arouse any one, shouldered his pack and went off grumbling. Then Joyce climbed down and walked slowly up the gravelled path to the house. Cousin Kate had just come back from Tours in the pony cart, and was waiting in the door to see if Gabriel had all the bundles that she had brought out with her.

Joyce followed her admiringly into the house. She wished that she could grow up to look

exactly like Cousin Kate, and wondered if she
would ever wear such stylish silk-lined skirts,
and catch them up in such an airy, graceful
way when she ran up-stairs; and if she would
ever have a Paris hat with long black feathers,
and always wear a bunch of sweet violets on
her coat.

She looked at herself in Cousin Kate's mir-
ror as she passed it, and sighed. "Well, I am
better-looking than when I left home," she
thought. "That's one comfort. My face isn't
freckled now, and my hair is more becoming
this way than in tight little pigtails, the way
I used to wear it."

Cousin Kate, coming up behind her, looked
over her head and smiled at the attractive re-
flection of Joyce's rosy cheeks and straightfor-
ward gray eyes. Then she stopped suddenly
and put her arms around her, saying, "What's
the matter, dear? You have been crying."

"Nothing," answered Joyce, but there was
a quaver in her voice, and she turned her head
aside. Cousin Kate put her hand under the
resolute little chin, and tilted it until she could
look into the eyes that dropped under her gaze.
"You have been crying," she said again, this

time in English, "crying because you are home sick. I wonder if it would not be a good occupation for you to open all the bundles that I got this afternoon. There is a saucepan in one, and a big spoon in the other, and all sorts of good things in the others, so that we can make some molasses candy here in my room, over the open fire. While it cooks you can curl up in the big armchair and listen to a fairy tale in the firelight. Would you like that, little one?"

"Oh, yes!" cried Joyce, ecstatically. "That's what they are doing at home this minute, I am sure. We always make candy every afternoon in the winter time."

Presently the saucepan was sitting on the coals, and Joyce's little pug nose was rapturously sniffing the odor of bubbling molasses. "I know what I'd like the story to be about," she said, as she stirred the delicious mixture with the new spoon. "Make up something about the big gate across the road, with the scissors on it."

Cousin Kate crossed the room, and sat down by the window, where she could look out and see the top of it.

"Let me think for a few minutes," she said.

" I have been very much interested in that old gate myself."

She thought so long that the candy was done before she was ready to tell the story; but while it cooled in plates outside on the window-sill, she drew Joyce to a seat beside her in the chimney-corner. With her feet on the fender, and the child's head on her shoulder, she began this story, and the firelight dancing on the walls, showed a smile on Joyce's contented little face.

CHAPTER II.

A NEW FAIRY TALE.

ONCE upon a time, on a far island of the sea, there lived a King with seven sons. The three eldest were tall and dark, with eyes like eagles, and hair like a crow's wing for blackness, and no princes in all the land were so strong and fearless as they. The three youngest sons were tall and fair, with eyes as blue as corn-flowers, and locks like the summer sun for brightness, and no princes in all the land were so brave and beautiful as they.

But the middle son was little and lorn; he was neither dark nor fair; he was neither handsome nor strong. So when the King saw that he never won in the tournaments nor led in the boar hunts, nor sang to his lute among the ladies of the court, he drew his royal robes around him, and henceforth frowned on Ethelried.

To each of his other sons he gave a portion of his kingdom, armor and plumes, a prancing charger, and a trusty sword ; but to Ethelried he gave nothing. When the poor Prince saw his brothers riding out into the world to win their fortunes, he fain would have followed. Throwing himself on his knees before the King, he cried, "Oh, royal Sire, bestow upon me also a sword and a steed, that I may up and away to follow my brethren."

But the King laughed him to scorn. "Thou a sword!" he quoth. "Thou who hast never done a deed of valor in all thy life! In sooth thou shalt have one, but it shall be one befitting thy maiden size and courage, if so small a weapon can be found in all my kingdom!"

Now just at that moment it happened that
the Court Tailor came into the room to measure
the King for a new mantle of ermine. Forth-
with the grinning Jester began shrieking with
laughter, so that the bells upon his motley cap
were all set a-jangling.

"What now, Fool?" demanded the King.

"I did but laugh to think the sword of Ethelried had been so quickly found," responded the
Jester, and he pointed to the scissors hanging
from the Tailor's girdle.

"By my troth," exclaimed the King, "it
shall be even as thou sayest!" and he com-
manded that the scissors be taken from the
Tailor, and buckled to the belt of Ethelried.

"Not until thou hast proved thyself a prince
with these, shalt thou come into thy kingdom,"
he swore with a mighty oath. "Until that far
day, now get thee gone!"

So Ethelried left the palace, and wandered
away over mountain and moor with a heavy
heart. No one knew that he was a prince;
no fireside offered him welcome; no lips gave
him a friendly greeting. The scissors hung
useless and rusting by his side.

One night as he lay in a deep forest, too

unhappy to sleep, he heard a noise near at hand in the bushes.   By the light of the moon he saw that a ferocious wild beast had been caught in a hunter's snare, and was struggling to free itself from the heavy net. His first thought was to slay the animal, for he had had no meat for many days.   Then he bethought himself that he had no weapon large enough.

While he stood gazing at the struggling beast, it turned to him with such a beseeching look in its wild eyes, that he was moved to pity.

"Thou shalt have thy liberty," he cried, "even though thou shouldst rend me in pieces the moment thou art free.   Better dead than this craven life to which my father hath doomed me!"

So he set to work with the little scissors to cut the great ropes of the net in twain.   At first each strand seemed as hard as steel, and the blades of the scissors were so rusty and dull that he could scarcely move them.   Great beads of sweat stood out on his brow as he bent himself to the task.

Presently, as he worked, the blades began to grow sharper and sharper, and brighter and brighter, and longer and longer. By the time that the last rope was cut the scissors were as sharp as a broadsword, and half as long as his body.

At last he raised the net to let the beast go free. Then he sank on his knees in astonishment. It had suddenly disappeared, and in its place stood a beautiful Fairy with filmy wings, which shone like rainbows in the moonlight.

"Prince Ethelried," she said in a voice that was like a crystal bell's for sweetness, "dost thou not know that thou art in the domain of a frightful Ogre? It was he who changed me into the form of a wild beast, and set the snare to capture me. But for thy fearlessness and faithful perseverance in the task which thou didst in pity undertake, I must have perished at dawn."

At this moment there was a distant rumbling as of thunder. "'Tis the Ogre!" cried the Fairy. "We must hasten." Seizing the scissors that lay on the ground where Ethelried had dropped them, she opened and shut them several times, exclaiming:

> "Scissors, grow a giant's height
> And save us from the Ogre's might!"

Immediately they grew to an enormous size, and, with blades extended, shot through the tangled thicket ahead of them, cutting down everything that stood in their way, — bushes, stumps, trees, vines ; nothing could stand before the fierce onslaught of those mighty blades.

The Fairy darted down the path thus opened up, and Ethelried followed as fast as he could, for the horrible roaring was rapidly coming nearer. At last they reached a wide chasm that bounded the Ogre's domain. Once across that, they would be out of his power, but it seemed impossible to cross. Again the Fairy touched the scissors, saying :

> " Giant scissors, bridge the path,
> And save us from the Ogre's wrath."

Again the scissors grew longer and longer, until they lay across the chasm like a shining bridge. Ethelried hurried across after the Fairy, trembling and dizzy, for the Ogre was now almost upon them. As soon as they were safe on the other side, the Fairy blew upon the scissors, and, presto, they became shorter and shorter until they were only the length of an ordinary sword.

"Here," she said, giving them into his hands; "because thou wast persevering and fearless in setting me free, these shall win for thee thy heart's desire. But remember that thou canst not keep them sharp and shining, unless they are used at least once each day in some unselfish service."

Before he could thank her she had vanished, and he was left in the forest alone. He could see the Ogre standing powerless to hurt him, on the other side of the chasm, and gnashing his teeth, each one of which was as big as a millstone.

The sight was so terrible, that he turned on his heel, and fled away as fast as his feet could carry him. By the time he reached the edge of the forest he was very tired, and ready to faint from hunger. His heart's greatest desire being for food, he wondered if the scissors could obtain it for him as the Fairy had promised. He had spent his last coin and knew not where to go for another.

Just then he spied a tree, hanging full of great, yellow apples. By standing on tiptoe he could barely reach the lowest one with his scissors. He cut off an apple, and was about

to take a bite, when an old Witch sprang out
of a hollow tree across the road.

"So you are the thief who has been stealing my gold apples all this last fortnight!" she
exclaimed. "Well, you shall never steal again,
that I promise you. Ho, Frog-eye Fearsome,
seize on him and drag him into your darkest
dungeon!"

At that, a hideous-looking fellow, with eyes
like a frog's, green hair, and horrid clammy
webbed fingers, clutched him before he could
turn to defend himself. He was thrust into
the dungeon and left there all day.

At sunset, Frog-eye Fearsome opened the
door to slide in a crust and a cup of water,
saying in a croaking voice, "You shall be
hanged in the morning, hanged by the neck
until you are quite dead." Then he stopped
to run his webbed fingers through his damp
green hair, and grin at the poor captive Prince,
as if he enjoyed his suffering. But the next
morning no one came to take him to the
gallows, and he sat all day in total darkness.
At sunset Frog-eye Fearsome opened the door
again to thrust in another crust and some water
and say, "In the morning you shall be drowned;

drowned in the Witch's mill-pond with a great stone tied to your heels."

Again the croaking creature stood and gloated over his victim, then left him to the silence of another long day in the dungeon. The third day he opened the door and hopped in, rubbing his webbed hands together with fiendish pleasure, saying, "You are to have no food and drink to-night, for the Witch has thought of a far more horrible punishment for you. In the morning I shall surely come again, and then — beware!"

Now as he stopped to grin once more at the poor Prince, a Fly darted in, and, blinded by the darkness of the dungeon, flew straight into a spider's web, above the head of Ethelried.

"Poor creature!" thought Ethelried. "Thou shalt not be left a prisoner in this dismal spot while I have the power to help thee." He lifted the scissors and with one stroke destroyed the web, and gave the Fly its freedom.

As soon as the dungeon had ceased to echo with the noise that Frog-eye Fearsome made in banging shut the heavy door, Ethelried heard a low buzzing near his ear. It was the Fly, which had alighted on his shoulder.

"Let an insect in its gratitude teach you this," buzzed the Fly. "To-morrow, if you remain here, you must certainly meet your doom, for the Witch never keeps a prisoner past the third night. But escape is possible. Your prison door is of iron, but the shutter which bars the window is only of wood. Cut your way out at midnight, and I will have a friend in waiting to guide you to a place of safety. A faint glimmer of light on the opposite wall shows me the keyhole. I shall make my escape thereat and go to repay thy unselfish service to me. But know that the scissors move only when bidden in rhyme. Farewell."

The Prince spent all the following time until midnight, trying to think of a suitable verse to say to the scissors. The art of rhyming had been neglected in his early education, and it was not until the first cock-crowing began that he succeeded in making this one :

> "Giant scissors, serve me well,
> And save me from the Witch's spell!"

As he uttered the words the scissors leaped out of his hand, and began to cut through the

wooden shutters as easily as through a cheese
In a very short time the Prince had crawled
through the opening.   There he stood, outside
the dungeon, but it was a dark night and he
knew not which way to turn.

He could hear Frog-eye Fearsome snoring
like a tempest up in the watch-tower, and the
old Witch was talking in her sleep in seven
languages.   While he stood looking around
him in bewilderment, a Firefly alighted on
his arm.   Flashing its little lantern in the
Prince's face, it cried, "This way! My friend,
the Fly, sent me to guide you to a place of
safety.   Follow me and trust entirely to my
guidance."

The Prince flung his mantle over his shoulder, and followed on with all possible speed.
They stopped first in the Witch's orchard, and
the Firefly held its lantern up while the Prince
filled his pockets with the fruit.   The apples
were gold with emerald leaves, and the cherries
were rubies, and the grapes were great bunches
of amethyst.   When the Prince had filled his
pockets he had enough wealth to provide for all
his wants for at least a twelvemonth.

The Firefly led him on until they came to a

town where was a fine inn. There he left him, and flew off to report the Prince's safety to the Fly and receive the promised reward.

Here Ethelried stayed for many weeks, living like a king on the money that the fruit jewels brought him. All this time the scissors were becoming little and rusty, because he never once used them, as the Fairy bade him, in unselfish service for others. But one day he bethought himself of her command, and started out to seek some opportunity to help somebody.

Soon he came to a tiny hut where a sick man lay moaning, while his wife and children wept beside him. "What is to become of me?" cried the poor peasant. "My grain must fall and rot in the field from overripeness because I have not the strength to rise and harvest it; then indeed must we all starve."

Ethelried heard him, and that night, when the moon rose, he stole into the field to cut it down with the giant scissors. They were so rusty from long idleness that he could scarcely move them. He tried to think of some rhyme with which to command them; but it had been so long since he had done any thinking, except for his own selfish pleasure, that his brain refused to work.

However, he toiled on all night, slowly cutting down the grain stalk by stalk. Towards morning the scissors became brighter and sharper, until they finally began to open and shut of their own accord. The whole field was cut by sunrise. Now the peasant's wife had risen very early to go down to the spring and dip up some cool water for her husband to drink. She came upon Ethelried as he was cutting the last row of the grain, and fell on her knees to thank him. From that day the peasant and all his family were firm friends of Ethelried's, and would have gone through fire and water to serve him.

After that he had many adventures, and he was very busy, for he never again forgot what the Fairy had said, that only unselfish service each day could keep the scissors sharp and shining. When the shepherd lost a little lamb one day on the mountain, it was Ethelried who found it caught by the fleece in a tangle of cruel thorns. When he had cut it loose and carried it home, the shepherd also became his firm friend, and would have gone through fire and water to serve him.

The grandame whom ne supplied with fagots,
the merchant whom he rescued from robbers,
the King's councillor to whom he gave aid,
all became his friends.   Up and down the
land, to beggar or lord, homeless wanderer or
high-born dame, he gladly
gave unselfish service all
unsought, and such as he
helped straightway became
his friends.

Day by day the scissors
grew sharper and sharper
and ever more quick to spring
forward at his bidding.

One day a herald dashed
down the highway, shouting
through his silver trumpet
that a beautiful Princess had
been carried away by the
Ogre.   She was the only
child of the King of this country, and the
knights and nobles of all other realms and all
the royal potentates were prayed to come to
her rescue.   To him who could bring her back
to her father's castle should be given the throne
and kingdom, as well as the Princess herself.

So from far and near, indeed from almost every country under the sun, came knights and princes to fight the Ogre. One by one their brave heads were cut off and stuck on poles along the moat that surrounded the castle.

Still the beautiful Princess languished in her prison. Every night at sunset she was taken up to the roof for a glimpse of the sky, and told to bid good-by to the sun, for the next morning would surely be her last. Then she would wring her lily-white hands and wave a sad farewell to her home, lying far to the westward. When the knights saw this they would rush down to the chasm and sound a challenge to the Ogre.

They were brave men, and they would not have feared to meet the fiercest wild beasts, but many shrunk back when the Ogre came rushing out. They dared not meet in single combat, this monster with the gnashing teeth, each one of which was as big as a millstone.

Among those who drew back were Ethelried's brothers (the three that were dark and the three that were fair). They would not acknowledge their fear. They said, " We are

THE PRINCESS.

only waiting to lay some wily plan to capture the Ogre."

After several days Ethelried reached the place on foot. "See him," laughed one of the brothers that was dark to one that was fair. "He comes afoot; no prancing steed, no waving plumes, no trusty sword; little and lorn, he is not fit to be called a brother to princes."

But Ethelried heeded not their taunts. He dashed across the drawbridge, and, opening his scissors, cried:

"Giant scissors, rise in power!
Grant me my heart's desire this hour!"

The crowds on the other side held their breath as the Ogre rushed out, brandishing a club as big as a church steeple. Then Whack! Bang! The blows of the scissors, warding off the blows of the mighty club, could be heard for miles around.

At last Ethelried became so exhausted that he could scarcely raise his hand, and it was plain to be seen that the scissors could not do battle much longer. By this time a great many people, attracted by the terrific noise, had come running up to the moat. The news had spread far and wide that Ethelried was in danger ; so every one whom he had ever served dropped whatever he was doing, and ran to the scene of the battle. The peasant was there, and the shepherd, and the lords and beggars and high-born dames, all those whom Ethelried had ever befriended.

As they saw that the poor Prince was about to be vanquished, they all began a great lamentation, and cried out bitterly.

" He saved my harvest," cried one. " He found my lamb," cried another. " He showed me a greater kindness still," shouted a third. And so they went on, each telling of some unselfish service that the Prince had rendered him. Their voices all joined at last into such a roar of gratitude that the scissors were given fresh strength on account of it. They grew longer and longer, and stronger and stronger, until with one great swoop they sprang forward and cut the ugly old Ogre's head from his shoulders.

Every cap was thrown up, and such cheering rent the air as has never been heard since They did not know his name, they did not know that he was Prince Ethelried, but they

knew by his valor that there was royal blood
in his veins. So they all cried out long and
loud : " *Long live the Prince ! Prince Ciseaux !* "

Then the King stepped down from his throne
and took off his crown to give to the conqueror,
but Ethelried put it aside.

" Nay," he said. " The only kingdom that I
crave is the kingdom of a loving heart and a
happy fireside. Keep all but the Princess."

So the Ogre was killed, and the Prince came
into his kingdom that was his heart's desire.
He married the Princess, and there was feasting
and merrymaking for seventy days and seventy
nights, and they all lived happily ever after.

When the feasting was over, and the guests
had all gone to their homes, the Prince pulled
down the house of the Ogre and built a new
one. On every gable he fastened a pair of
shining scissors to remind himself that only
through unselfish service to others comes the
happiness that is highest and best.

Over the great entrance gate he hung the
ones that had served him so valiantly, saying,
" Only those who belong to the kingdom of
loving hearts and happy homes can ever enter
here."

One day the old King, with the brothers of Ethelried (the three that were dark and the three that were fair), came riding up to the portal.   They thought to share in Ethelried's fame and splendor.   But the scissors leaped from their place and snapped so angrily in their faces that they turned their horses and fled.

Then the scissors sprang back to their place again to guard the portal of Ethelried, and, to this day, only those who belong to the kingdom of loving hearts may enter the Gate of the Giant Scissors

CHAPTER III.

THAT was the tale of the giant scissors as it was told to Joyce in the pleasant fire-lighted room; but behind the great gates the true story went on in a far different way.

Back of the Ciseaux house was a dreary field, growing drearier and browner every moment as the twilight deepened; and across its rough furrows a tired boy was stumbling wearily homeward. He was not more than nine years old, but the careworn expression of his thin white face might have belonged to a little old man of ninety. He was driving two unruly goats towards the house. The chase they led him would have been a laughable sight, had he not looked so small and forlorn plodding along in his clumsy wooden shoes, and a peasant's blouse of blue cotton, several sizes too large for his thin little body.

47

The anxious look in his eyes changed to one of fear as he drew nearer the house. At the sound of a gruff voice bellowing at him from the end of the lane, he winced as if he had been struck.

"Ha, there, Jules! 1hou lazy vagabond! Late again! Canst thou never learn that I am not to be kept waiting?"

"But, Brossard," quavered the boy in his shrill, anxious voice, "it was not my fault, indeed it was not. The goats were so stubborn to-night. They broke through the hedge, and I had to chase them over three fields."

"Have done with thy lying excuses," was the rough answer. "Thou shalt have no supper to-night. Maybe an empty stomach will teach thee when my commands fail. Hasten and drive the goats into the pen."

There was a scowl on Brossard's burly red face that made Jules's heart bump up in his throat. Brossard was only the caretaker of the Ciseaux place, but he had been there for twenty years, — so long that he felt himself the master. The real master was in Algiers nearly all the time. During his absence the great house was closed, excepting the kitchen and two rooms above it. Of these Brossard had one and Henri the other. Henri was the cook; a slow, stupid old man, not to be jogged out of either his good-nature or his slow gait by anything that Brossard might say.

Henri cooked and washed and mended, and hoed in the garden. Brossard worked in the fields and shaved down the expenses of their living closer and closer. All that was thus saved fell to his share, or he might not have watched the expenses so carefully.

Much saving had made him miserly. Old Therese, the woman with the fish-cart, used to say that he was the stingiest man in all Tour-raine. She ought to know, for she had sold him a fish every Friday during all those twenty years, and he had never once failed to quarrel about the price. Five years had gone by since the master's last visit. Brossard and Henri were not likely to forget that time, for they had been awakened in the dead of night by a loud knocking at the side gate. When they opened it the sight that greeted them made them rub their sleepy eyes to be sure that they saw aright.

There stood the master, old Martin Ciseaux.

His hair and fiercely bristling mustache had turned entirely white since they had last seen him. In his arms he carried a child.

Brossard almost dropped his candle in his first surprise, and his wonder grew until he could hardly contain it, when the curly head raised itself from monsieur's shoulder, and the sleepy baby voice lisped something in a foreign tongue.

"By all the saints!" muttered Brossard, as he stood aside for his master to pass.

"It's my brother Jules's grandson," was the curt explanation that monsieur offered. "Jules is dead, and so is his son and all the family, — died in America. This is his son's son, Jules, the last of the name. If I choose to take him from a foreign poorhouse and give him shelter, it's nobody's business, Louis Brossard, but my own."

With that he strode on up the stairs to his room, the boy still in his arms. This sudden coming of a four-year-old child into their daily life made as little difference to Brossard and Henri as the presence of the four-months-old puppy. They spread a cot for him in Henri's room when the master went back to Algiers.

They gave him something to eat three times a day when they stopped for their own meals, and then went on with their work as usual.

It made no difference to them that he sobbed in the dark for his mother to come and sing him to sleep, — the happy young mother who had petted and humored him in her own fond American fashion. They could not understand his speech; more than that, they could not understand him. Why should he mope alone in the garden with that beseeching look of a lost dog in his big, mournful eyes? Why should he not play and be happy, like the neighbor's children or the kittens or any other young thing that had life and sunshine?

Brossard snapped his fingers at him sometimes at first, as he would have done to a playful animal; but when Jules drew back, frightened by his foreign speech and rough voice, he began to dislike the timid child. After awhile he never noticed him except to push him aside or to find fault.

It was from Henri that Jules picked up whatever French he learned, and it was from Henri also that he had received the one awkward caress, and the only one, that his desolate little heart had known in all the five loveless years that he had been with them.

A few months ago Brossard had put him out in the field to keep the goats from straying away from their pasture, two stubborn crea-tures, whose self-willed wanderings had brought many a scolding down on poor Jules's head. To-night he was unusually unfortunate, for added to the weary chase they had led him was this stern command that he should go to bed without his supper.

He was about to pass into the house, shiver-ing and hungry, when Henri put his head out at the window. "Brossard," he called, "there isn't enough bread for supper; there's just this dry end of a loaf. You should have bought as I told you, when the baker's cart stopped here this morning."

Brossard slowly measured the bit of hard, black bread with his eye, and, seeing that there was not half enough to satisfy the appetites of two hungry men, he grudgingly drew a franc from his pocket.

"Here, Jules," he called. "Go down to the bakery, and see to it that thou art back by the time that I have milked the goats, or thou shalt go to bed with a beating, as well as supperless. Stay!" he added, as Jules turned to go. "I have a mind to eat white bread to-night instead of black. It will cost an extra sou, so be careful to count the change. It is only once or so in a twelvemonth," he muttered to himself as an excuse for his extravagance.

It was half a mile to the village, but down hill all the way, so that Jules reached the bakery in a very short time.

Several customers were ahead of him, how-ever, and he awaited his turn nervously. When he left the shop an old lamplighter was going down the street with torch and ladder, leaving a double line of twinkling lights in his wake, as he disappeared down the wide "Paris road." Jules watched him a moment, and then ran rapidly on. For many centuries the old village of St. Symphorien had echoed with the clatter of wooden shoes on its ancient cobblestones; but never had foot-falls in its narrow, crooked streets kept time to the beating of a lonelier little heart.

The officer of Customs, at his window beside the gate that shuts in the old town at night, nodded in a surly way as the boy hurried

past. Once outside the gate, Jules walked
more slowly, for the road began to wind up-hill.
Now he was out again in the open country,
where a faint light lying over the frosty fields
showed that the moon was rising.

Here and there lamps shone from the windows of houses along the road; across the
field came the bark of a dog, welcoming his
master; two old peasant women passed him in
a creaking cart on their glad way home.

At the top of the hill Jules stopped to take
breath, leaning for a moment against the stone
wall. He was faint from hunger, for he had
been in the fields since early morning, with
nothing for his midday lunch but a handful
of boiled chestnuts. The smell of the fresh
bread tantalized him beyond endurance. Oh,
to be able to take a mouthful, — just one little
mouthful of that brown, sweet crust!

He put his face down close, and shut his
eyes, drawing in the delicious odor with long,
deep breaths. What bliss it would be to have
that whole loaf for his own, — he, little Jules,
who was to have no supper that night! He
held it up in the moonlight, hungrily looking
at it on every side. There was not a broken

place to be found anywhere on its surface ; not one crack in all that hard, brown glaze of crust, from which he might pinch the tiniest crumb.

For a moment a mad impulse seized him to tear it in pieces, and eat every scrap, regardless of the reckoning with Brossard afterwards. But it was only for a moment. The memory of his last beating stayed his hand. Then, fearing to dally with temptation, lest it should master him, he thrust the bread under his arm, and ran every remaining step of the way home.

Brossard took the loaf from him, and pointed with it to the stairway, — a mute command for Jules to go to bed at once. Tingling with a sense of injustice, the little fellow wanted to shriek out in all his hunger and misery, defying this monster of a man ; but a struggling sparrow might as well have tried to turn on the hawk that held it. He clenched his hands to keep from snatching something from the table, set out so temptingly in the kitchen, but he dared not linger even to look at it. With a feeling of utter helplessness he passed it in silence, his face white and set.

Dragging his tired feet slowly up the stairs, he went over to the casement window, and swung it open; then, kneeling down, he laid his head on the sill, in the moonlight. Was it his dream that came back to him then, or only a memory? He could never be sure, for if it were a memory, it was certainly as strange as any dream, unlike anything he had ever known in his life with Henri a n d Brossard. Night after night he had comforted himself with the picture that it brought before him.

He could see a little white house in the middle of a big lawn. There were vines on the porches, and it must have been early in the evening, for the fireflies were beginning to twinkle over the lawn. And the grass had just been cut, for the air was sweet with the smell of it. A woman, standing on the steps under the vines, was calling "Jules, Jules, it is time to come in, little son!"

But Jules, in his white dress and shoulder

knots of blue ribbon, was toddling across the lawn after a firefly.

Then she began to call him another way. Jules had a vague idea that it was a part of some game that they sometimes played together. It sounded like a song, and the words were not like any that he had ever heard since he came to live with Henri and Brossard.   He could not forget them, though, for had they not sung themselves through that beautiful dream every time he had it ?

> " Little Boy Blue, oh, where are you ?
> O, where are you-u-u-u ? "

He only laughed in the dream picture and ran on after the firefly.   Then a man came running after him, and, catching him, tossed him up laughingly, and carried him to the house on his shoulder.

Somebody held a glass of cool, creamy milk for him to drink, and by and by he was in a little white night-gown in the woman's lap. His head was nestled against her shoulder, and he could feel her soft lips touching him on cheeks and eyelids and mouth, before she began to sing :

"Oh, little Boy Blue, lay by your horn,
    And mother will sing of the cows and the corn,
    Till the stars and the angels come to keep
    Their watch, where my baby lies fast asleep."

Now all of a sudden Jules knew that there was another kind of hunger worse than the longing for bread. He wanted the soft touch of those lips again on his mouth and eyelids, the loving pressure of those restful arms, a thousand times more than he had wished for the loaf that he had just brought home. Two hot tears, that made his eyes ache in their slow gathering, splashed down on the window-sill.

Down below Henri opened the kitchen door and snapped his fingers to call the dog. Looking out, Jules saw him set a plate of bones on the step. For a moment he listened to the animal's contented crunching, and then crept across the room to his cot, with a little moan. "O-o-oh — o-oh!" he sobbed. "Even the dog has more than I have, and I'm *so* hungry!" He hid his head awhile in the old quilt; then he raised it again, and, with the tears streaming down his thin little face, sobbed in a heart-broken whisper: "Mother! Mother! Do you know how hungry I am?"

A clatter of knives and forks from the kitchen below was the only answer, and he dropped despairingly down again.

" She's so far away she can't even hear me!" he moaned. " Oh, if I could only be dead, too!"

He lay there, crying, till Henri had finished washing the supper dishes and had put them clumsily away. The rank odor of tobacco, stealing up the stairs, told him that Brossard had settled down to enjoy his evening pipe. Through the casement window that was still ajar came the faint notes of an accordeon from Monsieur Gréville's garden, across the way. Gabriel, the coachman, was walking up and down in the moonlight, playing a wheezy accompaniment to the only song he knew. Jules did not notice it at first, but after awhile, when he had cried himself quiet, the faint melody began to steal soothingly into his consciousness. His eyelids closed drowsily, and then the accordeon seemed to be singing something to him. He could not understand at first, but just as he was dropping off to sleep he heard it quite clearly :

" Till the stars and the angels come to keep
   Their watch, where my baby lies fast asleep."

Late in the night Jules awoke with a start, and sat up, wondering what had aroused him. He knew that it must be after midnight, for the moon was nearly down.   Henri was snoring. Suddenly such a strong feeling of hunger came over him, that he could think of nothing else. It was like a gnawing pain.   As if he were being led by some power outside of his own will, he slipped to the door of the room.   The little bare feet made no noise on the carpetless floor.   No mouse could have stolen down the stairs more silently than timid little Jules.   The latch of the kitchen door gave a loud click that made him draw back with a shiver of alarm ; but that was all.   After waiting one breathless minute, his heart beating like a trip-hammer, he went on into the pantry.

The moon was so far down now, that only a white glimmer of light showed him the faint outline of things ; but his keen little nose guided him.   There was half a cheese on the swinging shelf, with all the bread that had been left from supper.   He broke off great pieces of each in eager haste.   Then he found a crock of goat's milk.   Lifting it to his mouth, he drank with big, quick gulps until he had to

"IT FELL TO THE FLOOR WITH A CRASH."

stop for breath. Just as he was about to raise it to his lips again, some instinct of danger made him look up. There in the doorway stood Brossard, bigger and darker and more threatening than he had ever seemed before.

A frightened little gasp was all that the child had strength to give. He turned so sick and faint that his nerveless fingers could no longer hold the crock. It fell to the floor with a crash, and the milk spattered all over the pantry. Jules was too terrified to utter a sound. It was Brossard who made the out-cry. Jules could only shut his eyes and crouch down trembling, under the shelf. The next instant he was dragged out, and Brossard's merciless strap fell again and again on the poor shrinking little body, that writhed under the cruel blows.

Once more Jules dragged himself up-stairs to his cot, this time bruised and sore, too ex-hausted for tears, too hopeless to think of possible to-morrows.

Poor little prince in the clutches of the ogre! If only fairy tales might be true! If only some gracious spirit of elfin lore might really come at such a time with its magic wand of healing! Then there would be no more little desolate hearts, no more grieved little faces with undried tears upon them in all the earth. Over every threshold where a child's wee feet had pattered in and found a home, it would hang its guardian Scissors of Avenging, so that only those who belong to the kingdom of loving hearts and gentle hands would ever dare to enter.

CHAPTER IV.

A LETTER AND A MEETING.

NEARLY a week later Joyce sat at her desk, hurrying to finish a letter before the postman's arrival.

"Dear Jack," it began.

"You and Mary will each get a letter this week. Hers is the fairy tale that Cousin Kate told me, about an old gate near here. I wrote it down as well as I could remember. I wish you could see that gate. It gets more interesting every day, and I'd give most anything to see what lies on the other side. Maybe I shall soon, for Marie has a way of finding out anything she wants to know. Marie is my new maid. Cousin Kate went to Paris last week, to be gone until nearly Christmas, so she got Marie to take care of me.

"It seems so odd to have somebody button my boots and brush my hair, and take me out to walk as if I were a big doll. I have to be very dignified and act as if I had always been used to such things. I believe

Marie would be shocked to death if she knew that I had ever washed dishes, or pulled weeds out of the pavement, or romped with you in the barn.

"Yesterday when we were out walking I got so tired of acting as if I were a hundred years old, that I felt as if I should scream. 'Marie,' I said, 'I've a mind to throw my muff in the fence-corner and run and hang on behind that wagon that's going down-hill.' She had no idea that I was in earnest. She just smiled very politely and said, 'Oh, mademoiselle, impossible! How you Americans do love to jest.' But it was no joke. You can't imagine how stupid it is to be with nobody but grown people all the time. I'm fairly aching for a good old game of hi spy or prisoner's base with you. There is nothing at all to do, but to take poky walks.

"Yesterday afternoon we walked down to the river. There's a double row of trees along it on this side, and several benches where people can wait for the tram-cars that pass down this street and then across the bridge into Tours. Marie found an old friend of hers sitting on one of the benches, — such a big fat woman, and oh, such a gossip! Marie said she was tired, so we sat there a long time. Her friend's name is Clotilde Robard. They talked about everybody in St. Symphorien.

"Then I gossiped, too. I asked Clotilde Robard if she knew why the gate with the big scissors was never opened any more. She told me that she used to be one of the maids there, before she married the spice-monger and was Madame Robard. Years before she went to live there, when the old Monsieur Ciseaux died, there

OUT WITH MARIE.

was a dreadful quarrel about some money. The son that got the property told his brother and sister never to darken his doors again.

"They went off to America, and that big front gate has never been opened since they passed out of it. Clotilde says that some people say that they put a curse on it, and something awful will happen to the first one who dares to go through. Isn't that interesting?

"The oldest son, Mr. Martin Ciseaux, kept up the place for a long time, just as his father had done, but he never married. All of a sudden he shut up the house, sent away all the servants but the two who take care of it, and went off to Algiers to live. Five years ago he came back to bring his little grand-nephew, but nobody has seen him since that time.

"Clotilde says that an orphan asylum would have been a far better home for Jules (that is the boy's name), for Brossard, the caretaker, is so mean to him. Doesn't that make you think of Prince Ethelried in the fairy tale? 'Little and lorn; no fireside welcomed him and no lips gave him a friendly greeting.'

"Marie says that she has often seen Jules down in the field, back of his uncle's house, tending the goats. I hope that I may see him sometime.

"Oh, dear, the postman has come sooner than I expected. He is talking down in the hall now, and if I do not post this letter now it will miss the evening train and be too late for the next mail steamer. Tell mamma that I will answer all her questions about my lessons and clothes next week. Oceans of love to everybody in the dear little brown house."

Hastily scrawling her name, Joyce ran out into the hall with her letter. "Anything for me?" she asked, anxiously, leaning over the banister to drop the letter into Marie's hand. "One, mademoiselle," was the answer. "But it has not a foreign stamp."

"Oh, from Cousin Kate!" exclaimed Joyce, tearing it open as she went back to her room. At the door she stooped to pick up a piece of paper that had dropped from the envelope. It crackled stiffly as she unfolded it.

"Money!" she exclaimed in surprise. "A whole twenty franc note. What could Cousin Kate have sent it for?" The last page of the letter explained.

"I have just remembered that December is not very far off, and that whatever little Christmas gifts we send home should soon be started on their way. Enclosed you will find twenty francs for your Christmas shopping. It is not much, but we are too far away to send anything but the simplest little remembrances, things that will not be spoiled in the mail, and on which little or no duty need be paid. You might buy one article each day, so that there will be some purpose in your walks into Tours.

"I am sorry that I can not be with you on Thanksgiving Day. We will have to drop it from our calendar this year; not the thanksgiving itself, but the turkey and mince pie part. Suppose you take a few francs to give yourself some little treat to mark the day. I hope my dear little girl will not be homesick all by herself. I never should have left just at this time if it had not been very necessary."

Joyce smoothed out the bank-note and looked at it with sparkling eyes. Twenty whole francs! The same as four dollars! All the money that she had ever had in her whole life put together would not have amounted to that much. Dimes were scarce in the little brown house, and even pennies seldom found their way into the children's hands when five pairs of little feet were always needing shoes, and five healthy appetites must be satisfied daily.

All the time that Joyce was pinning her treasure securely in her pocket and putting on her hat and jacket, all the time that she was walking demurely down the road with Marie, she was planning different ways in which to spend her fortune.

"Mademoiselle is very quiet," ventured Marie, remembering that one of her duties was to keep up an improving conversation with her little mistress.

"Yes," answered Joyce, half impatiently; "I've got something so lovely to think about, that I'd like to go back and sit down in the garden and just think and think until dark, without being interrupted by anybody."

This was Marie's opportunity. "Then mademoiselle might not object to stopping in the garden of the villa which we are now approaching," she said. "My friend, Clotilde Robard, is housekeeper there, and I have a very important message to deliver to her."

Joyce had no objection. "But, Marie," she said, as she paused at the gate, "I think I'll not go in. It is so lovely and warm out here in the sun that I'll just sit here on the steps and wait for you."

Five minutes went by and then ten. By that time Joyce had decided how to spend every centime in the whole twenty francs, and Marie had not returned. Another five minutes went by. It was dull, sitting there facing the lonely highway, down which no one ever seemed to pass. Joyce stood up, looked all around, and then slowly sauntered down the road a short distance.

Here and there in the crevices of the wall

blossomed a few hardy wild flowers, which Joyce began to gather as she walked. "I'll go around this bend in the road and see what's there," she said to herself. "By that time Marie will surely be done with her messages."

No one was in sight in any direction, and feeling that no one could be in hearing distance, either, in such a deserted place, she began to sing. It was an old Mother Goose rhyme that she hummed over and over, in a low voice at first, but louder as she walked on.

Around the bend in the road there was nothing to be seen but a lonely field where two goats were grazing. On one side of it was a stone wall, on two others a tall hedge, but the side next her sloped down to the road, unfenced.

Joyce, with her hands filled with the yellow wild flowers, stood looking around her, sing-ing the old rhyme, the song that she had taught the baby to sing before he could talk plainly :

"Little Boy Blue, come blow your horn,
The sheep's in the meadow, the cow's in the corn.
Little Blue Blue, oh, where are you?
Oh, where are you-u-u-u?"

The gay little voice that had been rising higher and higher, sweet as any bird's, stopped suddenly in mid-air; for, as if in answer to her call, there was a rustling just ahead of her, and a boy who had been lying on his back, looking at the sky, slowly raised himself out of the grass.

For an instant Joyce was startled; then see- ing by his wooden shoes and old blue cotton blouse that he was only a little peasant watch- ing the goats, she smiled at him with a pleasant good morning.

He did not answer, but came towards her with a dazed expression on his face, as if he were groping his way through some strange dream. "It is time to go in!" he exclaimed, as if repeating some lesson learned long ago, and half forgotten.

Joyce stared at him in open-mouthed aston- ishment. The little fellow had spoken in Eng- lish. "Oh, you must be Jules," she cried. "Aren't you? I've been wanting to find you for ever so long."

The boy seemed frightened, and did not answer, only looked at her with big, troubled eyes. Thinking that she had made a mistake,

"HE CAME TOWARDS HER WITH A DAZED EXPRESSION
ON HIS FACE."

that she had not heard aright, Joyce spoke in French. He answered her timidly. She had not been mistaken; he was Jules; he had been asleep, he told her, and when he heard her singing, he thought it was his mother calling him as she used to do, and had started up expecting to see her at last. Where was she? Did mademoiselle know her? Surely she must if she knew the song.

It was on the tip of Joyce's tongue to tell him that everybody knew that song; that it was as familiar to the children at home as the chirping of crickets on the hearth or the sight of dandelions in the spring-time. But some instinct warned her not to say it. She was glad afterwards, when she found that it was sacred to him, woven in as it was with his one beautiful memory of a home. It was all he had, and the few words that Joyce's singing had startled from him were all that he remembered of his mother's speech.

If Joyce had happened upon him in any other way, it is doubtful if their acquaintance would have grown very rapidly. He was afraid of strangers; but coming as she did with the familiar song that was like an old friend, he

felt that he must have known her sometime, —
that other time when there was always a sweet
voice calling, and fireflies twinkled across a
dusky lawn.

Joyce was not in a hurry for Marie to come
now.   She had a hundred questions to ask, and
made the most of her time by talking very fast.
"Marie will be frightened," she told Jules,
"if she does not find me at the gate, and will
think that the gypsies have stolen me.   Then
she will begin to hunt up and down the road,
and I don't know what she would say if she
came and found me talking to a strange child
out in the fields, so I must hurry back.   I
am glad that I found you.   I have been wishing so long for somebody to play with, and
you seem like an old friend because you were
born in America.   I'm going to ask madame to ask Brossard to let you come over
sometime."

Jules watched her as she hurried away, running lightly down the road, her fair hair flying
over her shoulders and her short blue skirt
fluttering.   Once she looked back to wave her
hand.   Long after she was out of sight he still
stood looking after her, as one might gaze long-

ingly after some visitant from another world. Nothing like her had ever dropped into his life before, and he wondered if he should ever see her again.

CHAPTER V.

A THANKSGIVING BARBECUE.

"THIS doesn't seem a bit like Thanksgiving Day, Marie," said Joyce, plaintively, as she sat up in bed to take the early breakfast that her maid brought in, — a cup of chocolate and a roll.

"In our country the very minute you wake up you can *feel* that it is a holiday. Outdoors it's nearly always cold and gray, with everything covered with snow. Inside you can smell turkey and pies and all sorts of good spicy things. Here it is so warm that the windows are open and flowers blooming in the garden, and there isn't a thing to make it seem different from any other old day."

Here her grumbling was interrupted by a knock at the door, and Madame Gréville's maid, Berthé, came in with a message.

"Madame and monsieur intend spending the day in Tours, and since Mademoiselle Ware has written that Mademoiselle Joyce is to have no lessons on this American holiday, they will be pleased to have her accompany them in the carriage. She can spend the morning with them there or return immediately with Gabriel."

"Of course I want to go," cried Joyce. "I love to drive. But I'd rather come back here to lunch and have it by myself in the garden. Berthé, ask madame if I can't have it served in the little kiosk at the end of the arbor."

As soon as she had received a most gracious permission, Joyce began to make a little plan. It troubled her conscience somewhat, for she felt that she ought to mention it to madame, but she was almost certain that madame would object, and she had set her heart on carrying it out.

"I won't speak about it now," she said to herself, "because I am not *sure* that I am going to do it. Mamma would think it was all right, but foreigners are so queer about some things."

Uncertain as Joyce may have been about her future actions, as they drove towards town, no sooner had madame and monsieur stepped from the carriage, on the Rue Nationale, than she was perfectly sure.

"Stop at the baker's, Gabriel," she ordered as they turned homeward, then at the big grocery on the corner. "Cousin Kate told me to treat myself to something nice," she said apologetically to her conscience, as she gave up the twenty francs to the clerk to be changed.

If Gabriel wondered what was in the little parcels which she brought back to the carriage, he made no sign. He only touched his hat respectfully, as she gave the next order: "Stop where the road turns by the cemetery, Gabriel; at the house with the steps going up to an iron-barred gate. I'll be back in two or three minutes," she said, when she had reached it, and climbed from the carriage.

To his surprise, instead of entering the gate, she hurried on past it, around the bend in the road. In a little while she came running back, her shoes covered with damp earth, as if she had been walking in a freshly ploughed field.

If Gabriel's eyes could have followed her around that bend in the road, he would have seen a sight past his understanding : Mademoiselle Joyce running at the top of her speed to meet a little goatherd in wooden shoes and blue cotton blouse, — a common little peasant goatherd.

"It's Thanksgiving Day, Jules," she announced, gasping, as she sank down on the ground beside him. "We're the only Americans here, and everybody has gone off ; and Cousin Kate said to celebrate in some way. I'm going to have a dinner in the garden. I've bought a rabbit, and we'll dig a hole, and make a fire, and barbecue it the way Jack and I used to do at home. And we'll roast eggs in the ashes, and have a fine time. I've got a lemon tart and a little iced fruit-cake, too."

All this was poured out in such breathless haste, and in such a confusion of tongues, first a sentence of English and then a word of French, that it is no wonder that Jules grew bewildered in trying to follow her. She had to begin again at the beginning, and speak very slowly, in order to make him understand that it was a feast day of some kind, and that he, Jules, was invited to some sort of a strange, wonderful entertainment in Monsieur Gréville's garden. " But Brossard is away from home," said Jules, "and there is no one to watch the goats, and keep them from straying down the road. Still it would be just the same if he were home," he added, sadly. " He would not let me go, I am sure. I have never been out of sight of that roof since I first came here, except on errands to the village, when I had to run all the way back." He pointed to the peaked gables, adorned by the scissors of his crazy old ancestor.

" Brossard isn't your father," cried Joyce, indignantly, "nor your uncle, nor your cousin, nor anything else that has a right to shut you up that way. Isn't there a field with a fence all around it, that you could drive the goats into for a few hours?"

Jules shook his head.

" Well, I can't have my Thanksgiving spoiled for just a couple of old goats," exclaimed Joyce. "You'll have to bring them along, and we'll shut them up in the carriage-house. You come over in about an hour, and I'll be at the side gate waiting for you."

Joyce had always been a general in her small way. She made her plans and issued her orders both at home and at school, and the children accepted her leadership as a matter of course. Even if Jules had not been willing and anxious to go, it is doubtful if he could have mustered courage to oppose the arrangements that she made in such a masterful way; but Jules had not the slightest wish to object to anything whatsoever that Joyce might propose.

It is safe to say that the old garden had never before even dreamed of such a celebration as the one that took place that afternoon behind its moss-coated walls. The time-stained statue of Eve, which stood on one side of the fountain, looked across at the weather-beaten figure of Adam, on the other side, in stony-eyed surprise. The little marble satyr in the middle of the fountain, which had been grinning ever since its endless shower-bath began, seemed to grin wider than ever, as it watched the children's strange sport.

Jules dug the little trench according to

Joyce's directions, and laid the iron grating which she had borrowed from the cook across it, and built the fire underneath. "We ought to have something especially patriotic and Thanks-givingey," said Joyce, standing on one foot to consider. "Oh, now I know," she cried, after a moment's thought. "Cousin Kate has a lovely big silk flag in the top of her trunk. I'll run and get that, and then I'll recite the 'Landing of the Pilgrims' to you while the rabbit cooks."

Presently a savory odor began to steal along the winding paths of the garden, between the laurel-bushes, — a smell of barbecued meat sput-tering over the fire. Above the door of the little kiosk, with many a soft swish of silken stirrings, hung the beautiful old flag. Then a clear little voice floated up through the pine-trees :

> "My country, 'tis of thee,
> Sweet land of liberty,
> Of thee I sing!"

All the time that Joyce sang, she was mov-ing around the table, setting out the plates and rattling cups and saucers. She could not keep a little quaver out of her voice, for, as she went on, all the scenes of all the times that she had sung that song before came crowding up in her memory. There were the Thanksgiving days in the church at home, and the Washington's birthdays at school, and two Decoration days, when, as a granddaughter of a veteran, she had helped scatter flowers over the soldiers' graves.

Somehow it made her feel so hopelessly far away from all that made life dear to be singing of that "sweet land of liberty" in a foreign country, with only poor little alien Jules for company.

Maybe that is why the boy's first lesson in patriotism was given so earnestly by his home-sick little teacher. Something that could not be put into words stirred within him, as, looking up at the soft silken flutterings of the old flag, he listened for the first time to the story of the Pilgrim Fathers.

The rabbit cooked slowly, so slowly that there was time for Jules to learn how to play mumble-peg while they waited. At last it was done, and Joyce proudly plumped it into the platter that had been waiting for it. Marie had already brought out a bountiful lunch, cold meats and salad and a dainty pudding. By the time that

Joyce had added her contribution to the feast, there was scarcely an inch of the table left uncovered. Jules did not know the names of half the dishes.

Not many miles away from that old garden, scattered up and down the Loire throughout all the region of fair Tourraine, rise the turrets of many an old château. Great banquet halls, where kings and queens once feasted, still stand as silent witnesses of a gay bygone court life; but never in any château or palace among them all was feast more thoroughly enjoyed than this impromptu dinner in the garden, where a little goatherd was the only guest.

It was an enchanted spot to Jules, made so by the magic of Joyce's wonderful gift of story-telling. For the first time in his life that he could remember, he heard of Santa Claus and Christmas trees, of Bluebeard and Aladdin's lamp, and all the dear old fairy tales that were so entrancing he almost forgot to eat.

Then they played that he was the prince, Prince Ethelried, and that the goats in the carriage-house were his royal steeds, and that Joyce was a queen whom he had come to visit.

But it came to an end, as all beautiful things

A LESSON IN PATRIOTISM.

must do. The bells in the village rang four, and Prince Ethelried started up as Cinderella must have done when the pumpkin coach disappeared. He was no longer a king's son; he was only Jules, the little goatherd, who must hurry back to the field before the coming of Brossard.

Joyce went with him to the carriage-house. Together they swung open the great door. Then an exclamation of dismay fell from Joyce's lips. All over the floor were scattered scraps of leather and cloth and hair, the kind used in upholstering. The goats had whiled away the hours of their imprisonment by chewing up the cushions of the pony cart.

Jules turned pale with fright. Knowing so little of the world, he judged all grown people by his knowledge of Henri and Brossard. "Oh, what will they do to us?" he gasped.

"Nothing at all," answered Joyce, bravely, although her heart beat twice as fast as usual as monsieur's accusing face rose up before her.

"It was all my fault," said Jules, ready to cry. "What must I do?" Joyce saw his distress, and with quick womanly tact recognized her duty as hostess. It would never do to let this, his first Thanksgiving Day, be clouded by a single unhappy remembrance. She would pretend that it was a part of their last game; so she waved her hand, and said, in a theatrical voice, " You forget, Prince Ethelried, that in the castle of Irmingarde she rules supreme. If it is the pleasure of your royal steeds to feed upon cushions they shall not be denied, even though they choose my own coach pillows, of gold-cloth and velour."

" But what if Gabriel should tell Brossard ? " questioned Jules, his teeth almost chattering at the mere thought.

"Oh, never mind, Jules," she answered, laughingly. " Don't worry about a little thing like that. I'll make it all right with madame as soon as she gets home."

Jules, with utmost faith in Joyce's power to do anything that she might undertake, drew a long breath of relief. Half a dozen times between the gate and the lane that led into the Ciseaux field, he turned around to wave his old cap in answer to the hopeful flutter of her little white handkerchief ; but when he was out of sight she went back to the carriage-

house and looked at the wreck of the cushions
with a sinking heart. After that second look,
she was not so sure of making it all right with
madame.

Going slowly up to her room, she curled up
in the window-seat to wait for the sound of the
carriage wheels. The blue parrots on the wall-
paper sat in their blue hoops in straight rows
from floor to ceiling, and hung all their dismal
heads. It seemed to Joyce as if there were
thousands of them, and that each one was more
unhappy than any of the others. The blue roses
on the bed-curtains, that had been in such gay
blossom a few hours before, looked ugly and
unnatural now.

Over the mantel hung a picture that had
been a pleasure to Joyce ever since she had
taken up her abode in this quaint blue room.
It was called "A Message from Noël," and
showed an angel flying down with gifts to fill
a pair of little wooden shoes that some child
had put out on a window-sill below. When
madame had explained that the little French
children put out their shoes for Saint Noël
to fill, instead of hanging stockings for Santa
Claus, Joyce had been so charmed with the

picture that she declared that she intended to
follow the French custom herself, this year.

Now, even the picture looked different, since
she had lost her joyful anticipations of Christmas. "It is all No-el to me now," she sobbed.
"No tree, no Santa Claus, and now, since the
money must go to pay for the goats' mischief, no
presents for anybody in the dear little brown
house at home, — not even mamma and the
baby!"

A big salty tear trickled down the side of
Joyce's nose and splashed on her hand; then
another one. It was such a gloomy ending for
her happy Thanksgiving Day. One consoling
thought came to her in time to stop the deluge
that threatened. "Anyway, Jules has had a
good time for once in his life." The thought
cheered her so much that when Marie came in
to light the lamps, Joyce was walking up and
down the room with her hands behind her back,
singing.

As soon as she was dressed for dinner she
went down-stairs, but found no one in the
drawing-room. A small fire burned cozily on
the hearth, for the November nights were growing chilly. Joyce picked up a book and tried

co read, but found herself looking towards the door fully as often as at the page before her. Presently she set her teeth together and swallowed hard, for there was a rustling in the hall. The portière was pushed aside and madame

 swept into the room in a dinner-gown of dark red velvet.

To Joyce's waiting eyes she seemed more imposing, more elegant, and more unapproachable than she had ever been before. At madame's entrance Joyce rose as usual, but when the red velvet train had swept on to a seat beside the fire, she still remained standing. Her lips seemed glued together after those first words of greeting.

"Be seated, mademoiselle," said the lady, with a graceful motion of her hand towards a chair. "How have you enjoyed your holiday?"

Joyce gave a final swallow of the choking

lump in her throat, and began her humble con-
fession that she had framed up-stairs among
the rows of dismal blue wall-paper parrots. She
started with Clotilde Robard's story of Jules,
told of her accidental meeting with him, of all
that she knew of his hard life with Brossard,
and of her longing for some one to play with.
Then she acknowledged that she had planned
the barbecue secretly, fearing that madame
would not allow her to invite the little goatherd.   At the conclusion, she opened the handkerchief which she had been holding tightly
clenched in her hand, and poured its contents
in the red velvet lap.

"There's all that is left of my Christmas
money," she said, sadly, "seventeen francs
and two sous.   If it isn't enough to pay for the
cushions, I'll write to Cousin Kate, and maybe
she will lend me the rest."

Madame gathered up the handful of coin,
and slowly rose.   "It is only a step to the carriage-house," she said.   "If you will kindly
ring for Berthé to bring a lamp we will look to
see how much damage has been done."

It was an unusual procession that filed down
the garden walk a few minutes later.   First

came Berthé, in her black dress and white cap, holding a lamp high above her head, and screwing her forehead into a mass of wrinkles as she peered out into the surrounding darkness. After her came madame, holding up her dress and stepping daintily along in her high-heeled little slippers. Joyce brought up the rear, stumbling along in the darkness of madame's large shadow, so absorbed in her troubles that she did not see the amused expression on the face of the grinning satyr in the fountain.

Eve, looking across at Adam, seemed to wink one of her stony eyes, as much as to say, " Humph ! Somebody else has been getting into trouble. There's more kinds of forbidden fruit than one ; pony-cart cushions, for instance."

Berthé opened the door, and madame stepped inside the carriage-house. With her skirts held high in both hands, she moved around among the wreck of the cushions, turning over a bit with the toe of her slipper now and then.

Madame wore velvet dinner-gowns, it is true, and her house was elegant in its fine old furnishings bought generations ago ; but only her dressmaker and herself knew how many times those gowns had been ripped and cleaned and remodelled. It was only constant housewifely skill that kept the antique furniture repaired and the ancient brocade hangings from falling into holes. None but a French woman, trained in petty economies, could have guessed how little money and how much thought was spent in keeping her table up to its high standard of excellence.

Now as she looked and estimated, counting the fingers of one hand with the thumb of the other, a wish stirred in her kind old heart that she need not take the child's money; but new cushions must be bought, and she must be just to herself before she could be generous to others. So she went on with her estimating and counting, and then called Gabriel to consult with him.

" Much of the same hair can be used again," she said, finally, " and the cushions were partly worn, so that it would not be right for you to have to bear the whole expense of new ones. I shall keep sixteen, — no, I shall keep only fifteen francs of your money, mademoiselle. I am sorry to take any of it, since you have been so frank with me; but you must see that it would not be justice for me to have to suffer in consequence of your fault. In France, children do nothing without the permission of their elders, and it would be well for you to adopt the same rule, my dear mademoiselle."

Here she dropped two francs and two sous into Joyce's hand. It was more than she had dared to hope for. Now there would be at least a little picture-book apiece for the children at home.

This time Joyce saw the grin on the satyr's face when they passed the fountain. She was smiling herself when they entered the house, where monsieur was waiting to escort them politely in to dinner.

CHAPTER VI.

JOYCE PLAYS GHOST.

MONSIEUR CISEAUX was coming home to live. Gabriel brought the news when he came back from market. He had met Henri on the road and heard it from him. Monsieur was coming home. That was all they knew; as to the day or the hour, no one could guess. That was the way with monsieur, Henri said. He was so peculiar one never knew what to expect.

Although the work of opening the great house was begun immediately, and a thorough cleaning was in progress from garret to cellar, Brossard did not believe that his master would really be at home before the end of the week. He made his own plans accordingly, although he hurried Henri relentlessly with the cleaning.

As soon as Joyce heard the news she made an excuse to slip away, and ran down to the field to Jules. She found him paler than

usual, and there wa\. swollen look about his
eyes that made her think that maybe he had
been crying.

"What's the matter?" she asked. "Aren't
you glad that your uncle is coming home?"

Jules gave a cautious glance over his shoulder
towards the house, and then looked up at Joyce.
Heretofore, some inward monitor of pride had
closed his lips about himself whenever he had
been with her, but, since the Thanksgiving Day
that had made them such firm friends, he had
wished every hour that he could tell her of his
troubles. He felt that she was the only person
in the world who took any interest in him.
Although she was only three years older than
himself, she had that motherly little way with
her that eldest daughters are apt to acquire
when there is a whole brood of little brothers
and sisters constantly claiming attention.

So when Joyce asked again, "What's the
matter, Jules?" with so much anxious sympathy in her face and voice, the child found
himself blurting out the truth.

"Brossard beat me again last night," he
exclaimed. Then, in response to her indignant
exclamation, he poured out the whole story of

his ill-treatment. "See here!" he cried, in conclusion, unbuttoning his blouse and baring his thin little shoulders. Great red welts lay across them, and one arm was blue with a big mottled bruise.

Joyce shivered and closed her eyes an instant to shut out the sight that brought the quick tears of sympathy.

"Oh, you poor little thing!" she cried. "I'm going to tell madame."

"No, don't!" begged Jules. "If Brossard ever found out that I had told anybody, I believe that he would half kill me. He punishes me for the least thing. I had no breakfast this morning because I dropped an old plate and broke it."

"Do you mean to say," cried Joyce, "that you have been out here in the field since sunrise without a bite to eat?"

Jules nodded.

"Then I'm going straight home to get you something." Before he could answer she was darting over the fields like a little flying squirrel.

"Oh, what if it were Jack!" she kept repeating as she ran. "Dear old Jack, beaten and starved, without anybody to love him or say a

kind word to him." The mere thought of such
misfortune brought a sob.

In a very few minutes Jules saw her coming
across the field again, more slowly this time,
for both hands were full, and without their aid
she had no way to steady the big hat that
flapped forward into her eyes at every step.
Jules eyed the food ravenously. He had not
known how weak and hungry he was until
then.

"It will not be like this when your uncle
comes home," said Joyce, as she watched the
big mouthfuls disappear down the grateful
little throat. Jules shrugged his shoulders,
answering tremulously, "Oh, yes, it will be lots
worse. Brossard says that my Uncle Martin
has a terrible temper, and that he turned his
poor sister and my grandfather out of the
house one stormy might. Brossard says he
shall tell him how troublesome I am, and
likely he will turn me out, too. Or, if he
doesn't do that, they will both whip me every
day."

Joyce stamped her foot. "I don't believe
it," she cried, indignantly. "Brossard is only
trying to scare you. Your uncle is an old man

now, so old that he must be sorry for the way he acted when he was young. Why, of course he must be," she repeated, "or he never would have brought you here when you were left a homeless baby. More than that, I believe he will be angry when he finds how you have been treated. Maybe he will send Brossard away when you tell him."

"I would not dare to tell him," said Jules, shrinking back at the bare suggestion.

"Then *I* dare," cried Joyce with flashing eyes. "I am not afraid of Brossard or Henri or your uncle, or any man that I ever knew. What's more, I intend to march over here just as soon as your uncle comes home, and tell him right before Brossard how you have been treated."

Jules gasped in admiration of such reckless courage. "Seems to me Brossard himself would be afraid of you if you looked at him that way." Then his voice sank to a whisper. "Brossard is afraid of one thing, I've heard him tell Henri so, and that is *ghosts*. They talk about them every night when the wind blows hard and makes queer noises in the chimney. Sometimes they are afraid to put out their candles for fear some evil spirit might be in the room."

"I'm glad he is afraid of something, the mean old thing!" exclaimed Joyce. For a few moments nothing more was said, but Jules felt comforted now that he had unburdened his long pent up little heart. He reached out for several blades of grass and began idly twisting them around his finger.

Joyce sat with her hands clasped over her knees, and a wicked little gleam in her eyes that boded mischief. Presently she giggled as if some amusing thought had occurred to her, and when Jules looked up inquiringly she began noiselessly clapping her hands together.

"I've thought of the best thing," she said. "I'll fix old Brossard now. Jack and I have played ghost many a time, and have even scared each other while we were doing it, because we were so frightful-looking. We put long sheets all over us and went about with pumpkin jack-o'-lanterns on our heads. Oh, we looked awful, all in white, with fire shining out of those hideous eyes and mouths. If I knew when Brossard was likely to whip you again, I'd suddenly appear on the scene and shriek out like a banshee and make him stop. Wouldn't it be lovely?" she cried, more carried away with the idea the longer she thought of it. "Why, it would be like acting our fairy story. You are the Prince, and I will be the giant scissors and rescue you from the Ogre. Now let me see if I can think of a rhyme for you to say whenever you need me."

Joyce put her hands over her ears and began to mumble something that had no meaning whatever for Jules: "Ghost — post — roast — toast, — no that will never do; need — speed deed, — no! Help — yelp (I wish I could make him yelp), — friend — spend — lend, — that's it. I shall try that."

There was a long silence, during which Joyce whispered to herself with closed eyes. "Now I've got it," she announced, triumphantly, "and it's every bit as good as Cousin Kate's:

> " Giant scissors, fearless friend,
> Hasten, pray, thy aid to lend.

"If you could just say that loud enough for me to hear I'd come rushing in and save you."

Jules repeated the rhyme several times, until

he was sure that he could remember it, and then Joyce stood up to go.

"Good-by, fearless friend," said Jules. "I wish I were brave like you." Joyce smiled in a superior sort of way, much flattered by the new title. Going home across the field she held her head a trifle higher than usual, and carried on an imaginary conversation with Brossard, in which she made him quail before her scathing rebukes.

Joyce did not take her usual walk that afternoon. She spent the time behind locked doors busy with paste, scissors, and a big muff-box, the best foundation she could find for a jack-o'-lantern. First she covered the box with white paper and cut a hideous face in one side, — great staring eyes, and a frightful grinning mouth. With a bit of wire she fastened a candle inside and shut down the lid.

"Looks too much like a box yet," she said, after a critical examination. "It needs some hair and a beard. Wonder what I can make it of." She glanced all around the room for a suggestion, and then closed her eyes to think Finally she went over to her bed, and, turning the covers back from one corner, began ripping a seam in the mattress. When the opening was wide enough she put in her thumb and finger and pulled out a handful of the curled hair. "I can easily put it back when I have used it, and sew up the hole in the mattress," she said to her conscience. "My! This is exactly what I needed."

The hair was mixed, white and black, coarse and curly as a negro's wool.

She covered the top of the pasteboard head with it, and was so pleased that she added long beard and fierce mustache to the already hideous mouth. When that was all done she took it into a dark closet and lighted the candle. The monster's head glared at her from the depth of the closet, and she skipped back and forth in front of it, wringing her hands in delight.

"Oh, if Jack could only see it! If he could

only see it!" she kept exclaiming. "It is better than any pumpkin head we ever made, and scary enough to throw old Brossard into a fit. I can hardly wait until it is dark enough to go over."

Meanwhile the short winter day drew on towards the close. Jules, out in the field with the goats, walked back and forth, back and forth, trying to keep warm. Brossard, who had gone five miles down the Paris road to bargain about some grain, sat comfortably in a little tobacco shop, with a pipe in his mouth and a glass and bottle on the table at his elbow. Henri was at home, still scrubbing and cleaning. The front of the great house was in order, with even the fires laid on all the hearths ready for lighting. Now he was scrubbing the back stairs. His brush bumped noisily against the steps, and the sound of its scouring was nearly drowned by the jerky tune which the old fellow sung through his nose as he worked.

A carriage drove slowly down the road and stopped at the gate with the scissors; then, in obedience to some command from within, the vehicle drove on to the smaller gate beyond. An old man with white hair and bristling

mustache slowly alighted. The master had
come home. He put out his hand as if to
ring the bell, then on second thought drew
a key from his pocket and fitted it in the
lock. The gate swung back and he passed
inside. The old house looked gray and forbidding in the dull light of the late afternoon.
He frowned up at it, and it frowned down on
him, standing there as cold and grim as itself.
That was his only welcome.

The doors and windows were all shut, so
that he caught only a faint sound of the
bump, thump of the scrubbing-brush as it
accompanied Henri's high-pitched tune down
the back stairs.

Without giving any warning of his arrival, he
motioned the man beside the coachman to follow with his trunk, and silently led the way
up-stairs. When the trunk had been unstrapped
and the man had departed, monsieur gave one
slow glance all around the room. It was in
perfect readiness for him. He set a match to
the kindling laid in the grate, and then closed
the door into the hall. The master had come
home again, more silent, more mysterious in
his movements than before.

Henri finished his scrubbing and his song, and, going down into the kitchen, began preparations for supper. A long time after, Jules came up from the field, put the goats in their place, and crept in behind the kitchen stove.

Then it was that Joyce, from her watch-tower of her window, saw Brossard driving home in the market-cart. "Maybe I'll have a chance to scare him while he is putting the horse up and feeding it," she thought. It was in the dim gloaming when she could easily slip along by the hedges without attracting attention. Bareheaded, and in breathless haste to reach the barn before Brossard, she ran down the road, keeping close to the hedge, along which the wind raced also, blowing the dead leaves almost as high as her head.

Slipping through a hole in the hedge, just as Brossard drove in at the gate, she ran into the barn and crouched down behind the door. There she wrapped herself in the sheet that she had brought with her for the purpose, and proceeded to strike a match to light the lantern. The first one flickered and went out. The second did the same. Brossard was calling angrily for Jules now, and she struck another match in nervous haste, this time touching the wick with it before the wind could interfere. Then she drew her dress over the lantern to hide the light.

"Wouldn't Jack enjoy this," she thought, with a daring little giggle that almost betrayed her hiding-place.

"I tell thee it is thy fault," cried Brossard's angry voice, drawing nearer the barn.

"But I tried," began Jules, timidly.

His trembling excuse was interrupted by Brossard, who had seized him by the arm. They were now on the threshold of the barn, which was as dark as a pocket inside.

Joyce, peeping through the crack of the door, saw the man's arm raised in the dim twilight outside. "Oh, he is really going to beat him," she thought, turning faint at the prospect. Then her indignation overcame every other feeling as she heard a heavy halter-strap whiz through the air and fall with a sickening blow across Jules's shoulders. She had planned a scene something like this while she worked away at the lantern that afternoon. Now she felt as if she were acting a part in some private theatrical perform ance. Jules's cry gave her the cue, and the courage to appear.

As the second blow fell across Jules's smarting shoulders, a low, blood-curdling wail came from the dark depths of the barn. Joyce had not practised that dismal moan of a banshee to no purpose in her ghost dances at home with Jack. It rose and fell and quivered and rose again in cadences of horror. There was something awful, something inhuman, in that fiendish, long-drawn shriek.

Brossard's arm fell to his side paralyzed with fear, as that same hoarse voice cried, solemnly : "Brossard, beware! Beware!" But worse than that voice of sepulchral warning was the white-sheeted figure, coming towards him with a wavering, ghostly motion, fire shooting from the demon-like eyes, and flaming from the hideous mouth.

Brossard sank on his knees in a shivering heap, and began crossing himself. His hair was upright with horror, and his tongue stiff. Jules knew who it was that danced around them in such giddy circles, first darting towards them with threatening gestures, and then gliding back to utter one of those awful, sickening wails. He knew that under that fiery head and wrapped in that spectral dress was his "fearless friend," who, according to promise, had hastened her aid to lend ; nevertheless, he was afraid of her himself. He had never imagined that anything could look so terrifying.

The wail reached Henri's ears and aroused his curiosity. Cautiously opening the kitchen door, he thrust out his head, and then nearly fell backward in his haste to draw it in again and slam the door. One glimpse of the ghost in the barnyard was quite enough for Henri.

Altogether the performance probably did not last longer than a minute, but each of the sixty seconds seemed endless to Brossard. With a final die-away moan Joyce glided towards the gate, delighted beyond measure with her success ; but her delight did not last long. Just as she turned the corner of the house, some one standing in the shadow of it clutched her. A strong arm was thrown around her, and a firm hand snatched the lantern, and tore the sheet away from her face.

It was Joyce's turn to be terrified. " Let me go ! " she shrieked, in English. With one des-

"'BROSSARD, BEWARE! BEWARE!'"

perate wrench she broke away, and by the light
of the grinning jack-o'-lantern saw who was her
raptor. She was face to face with Monsieur
Ciseaux.

"What does this mean?" he asked, severely.
"Why do you come masquerading here to
frighten my servants in this manner?"

For an instant Joyce stood speechless. Her
boasted courage had forsaken her. It was only
for an instant, however, for the rhyme that
she had made seemed to sound in her ears as
distinctly as if Jules were calling to her:

> "Giant scissors, fearless friend,
> Hasten, pray, thy aid to lend."

"I will be a fearless friend," she thought.
Looking defiantly up into the angry face she
demanded: "Then why do you keep such servants? I came because they needed to be
frightened, and I'm glad you caught me, for I
told Jules that I should tell you about them as
soon as you got home. Brossard has starved
and beaten him like a dog ever since he has
been here. I just hope that you will look at
the stripes and bruises on his poor little back.
He begged me not to tell, for Brossard said you

would likely drive him away, as you did your brother and sister. But even if you do, the neighbors say that an orphan asylum would be a far better home for Jules than this has been. I hope you'll excuse me, monsieur, I truly do, but I'm an American, and I can't stand by and keep still when I see anybody being abused, even if I am a girl, and it isn't polite for me to talk so to older people."

Joyce fired out the words as if they had been bullets, and so rapidly that monsieur could scarcely follow her meaning. Then, having relieved her mind, and fearing that maybe she had been rude in speaking so forcibly to such an old gentleman, she very humbly begged his pardon. Before he could recover from her rapid change in manner and her torrent of words, she reached out her hand, saying, in the meekest of little voices, "And will you please give me back those things, monsieur? The sheet is Madame Gréville's, and I've got to stuff that hair back in the mattress to-night."

Monsieur gave them to her, still too aston-ished for words. He had never before heard any child speak in such a way. This one seemed more like a wild, uncanny little sprite

than like any of the little girls he had known
heretofore.   Before he could recover from his
bewilderment, Joyce had gone.   " Good night,
monsieur," she called, as the gate clanged
behind her.

CHAPTER VII.

OLD "NUMBER THIRTY - ONE."

No sooner had the gate closed upon the subdued little ghost, shorn now of its terrors, than the old man strode forward to the place where Brossard crouched in the straw, still crossing himself. This sudden appearance of his master at such a time only added to Brossard's fright. As for Jules, his knees shook until he could scarcely stand.

Henri, his curiosity lending him courage, cautiously opened the kitchen door to peer out again. Emboldened by the silence, he flung the door wide open, sending a broad stream of lamplight across the little group in the barnyard. Without a word of greeting monsieur laid hold of the trembling Jules and drew him nearer the door. Throwing open the child's blouse, he examined the thin little shoulders, which shrank away as if to dodge some expected blow.

"Go to my room," was all the old man said to him. Then he turned fiercely towards Bros

sard. His angry tones reached Jules even after he had mounted the stairs and closed the door The child crept close to the cheerful fire, and, crouching down on the rug, waited in a shiver of nervousness for his uncle's step on the stair.

Meanwhile, Joyce, hurrying home all a-tingle with the excitement of her adventure, wondered anxiously what would be the result of it. Under cover of the dusk she slipped into the house unobserved. There was barely time to dress for dinner. When she made her appearance monsieur complimented her unusually red cheeks.

"Doubtless mademoiselle has had a fine promenade," he said.

"No," answered Joyce, with a blush that made them redder still, and that caused madame to look at her so keenly that she felt those sharp eyes must be reading her inmost thoughts. It disturbed her so that she upset the salt, spilled a glass of water, and started to eat her soup with a fork. She glanced in an embarrassed way from madame to monsieur, and gave a nervous little laugh.

"The little mademoiselle has been in mischief again," remarked monsieur, with a smile. "What is it this time?"

The smile was so encouraging that Joyce's determination not to tell melted away, and she began a laughable account of the afternoon's adventure. At first both the old people looked shocked. Monsieur shrugged his shoulders and pulled his gray beard thoughtfully. Madame threw up her hands at the end of each sentence like horrified little exclamation points. But when Joyce had told the entire story neither of them had a word of blame, because their sympathies were so thoroughly aroused for Jules.

"I shall ask Monsieur Ciseaux to allow the child to visit here sometimes," said madame, her kind old heart full of pity for the motherless little fellow; "and I shall also explain that it was only your desire to save Jules from ill treatment that caused you to do such an unusual thing. Otherwise he might think you too bold and too — well, peculiar, to be a fit playmate for his little nephew."

"Oh, was it really so improper and horrid of me, madame?" asked Joyce, anxiously.

Madame hesitated. "The circumstances were some excuse," she finally admitted. "But I certainly should not want a little daughter of mine to be out after dark by herself on such a wild errand. In this country a little girl would not think it possible to do such a thing."

Joyce's face was very sober as she arose to leave the room. "I do wish that I could be proper like little French girls," she said with a sigh.

Madame drew her towards her, kissing her on both cheeks. It was such an unusual thing for madame to do that Joyce could scarcely help showing some surprise. Feeling that the caress was an assurance that she was not in disgrace, as she had feared, she ran up-stairs, so light-hearted that she sang on the way.

As the door closed behind her, monsieur reached for his pipe, saying, as he did so, " She has a heart of gold, the little mademoiselle."

"Yes," assented madame; "but she is a strange little body, so untamed and original. I am glad that her cousin returns soon, for the responsibility is too great for my old shoulders. One never knows what she will do next."

Perhaps it was for this reason that madame took Joyce with her when she went to Tours next day. She felt safer when the child was in her sight.

"It is so much nicer going around with you than Marie," said Joyce, giving madame an affectionate little pat, as they stood before the entrance of a great square building, awaiting admission. "You take me to places that I

have never seen before. What place is this?"
She stooped to read the inscription on the
door-plate :

"LITTLE SISTERS OF THE POOR."

Before her question could be answered, the
door was opened by a wrinkled old woman, in a
nodding white cap, who led them into a recep-
tion-room at the end of the hall.

"Ask for Sister Denisa," said madame, "and
give her my name."

The old woman shuffled out of the room,
and madame, taking a small memorandum book
from her pocket, began to study it. Joyce sat
looking about her with sharp, curious glances.
She wondered if these little sisters of the poor
were barefoot beggar girls, who went about the
streets with ragged shawls over their heads,
and with baskets in their hands. In her lively
imagination she pictured row after row of such
unfortunate children, marching out in the morning, empty-handed, and creeping back at night
with the results of the day's begging. She did
not like to ask about them, however, and, in a
few minutes, her curiosity was satisfied without
the use of questions.

Sister Denisa entered the room. She was a beautiful woman, in the plain black habit and white head-dress of a sister of charity.

"Oh, they're nuns!" exclaimed Joyce, in a disappointed whisper. She had been hoping to see the beggar girls. She had often passed the convent in St. Symphorien, and caught glimpses of the nuns, through the high barred gate. She had wondered how it must feel to be shut away from the world; to see only the patient white faces of the other sisters, and to walk with meekly folded hands and downcast eyes always in the same old paths.

But Sister Denisa was different from the nuns that she had seen before. Some inward joy seemed to shine through her beautiful face and make it radiant. She laughed often, and there was a happy twinkle in her clear, gray eyes. When she came into the room, she seemed to bring the outdoors with her, there was such sunshine and fresh air in the cheeriness of her greeting.

Madame had come to visit an old pensioner of hers who was in the home. After a short conversation, Sister Denisa rose to lead the way to her. "Would the little mademoiselle

JOYCE AND SISTER DENISA.

like to go through the house while madame is engaged ? " asked the nun.

" Oh, yes, thank you," answered Joyce, who had found by this time that this home was not for little beggar girls, but for old men and women. Joyce had known very few old people in her short life, except her Grandmother Ware; and this grandmother was one of those dear, sunny old souls, whom everybody loves to claim, whether they are in the family or not. Some of Joyce's happiest days had been spent in her grandmother's country home, and the host of happy memories that she had stored up during those visits served to sweeten all her after life.

Old age, to Joyce, was associated with the most beautiful things that she had ever known : the warmest hospitality, the tenderest love, the cheeriest home-life. Strangers were in the old place now, and Grandmother Ware was no longer living, but, for her sake, Joyce held sacred every wrinkled face set round with snow-white hair, just as she looked tenderly on all old-fashioned flowers, because she had seen them first in her grandmother's garden.

Sister Denisa led the way into a large, sunny

room, and Joyce looked around eagerly. It was crowded with old men. Some were sitting idly on the benches around the walls, or dozing in chairs near the stove. Some smoked, some gathered around the tables where games of checkers and chess were going on; some gazed listlessly out of the windows. It was good to see how dull faces brightened, as Sister Denisa passed by with a smile for this group, a cheery word for the next. She stopped to brush the hair back from the forehead of an old paralytic, and pushed another man gently aside, when he blocked the way, with such a sweet-voiced "Pardon, little father," that it was like a caress. One white-haired old fellow, in his second childhood, reached out and caught at her dress, as she passed by.

Crossing a porch where were more old men sitting sadly alone, or walking sociably up and down in the sunshine, Sister Denisa passed along a court and held the door open for Joyce to enter another large room.

"Here is the rest of our family," she said. "A large one, is it not? Two hundred poor old people that nobody wants, and nobody cares what becomes of."

Joyce looked around the room and saw on every hand old age that had nothing beautiful, nothing attractive. "Were they beggars when they were little?" she asked.

"No, indeed," answered the nun. "That is the saddest part of it to me. Nearly all these poor creatures you see here once had happy homes of their own. That pitiful old body over by the stove, shaking with palsy, was once a gay, rich countess ; the invalid whom madame visits was a marquise. It would break your heart, mademoiselle, to hear the stories of some of these people, especially those who have been cast aside by ungrateful children, to whom their support has become a burden. Several of these women have prosperous grandchildren, to whom we have appealed in vain. There is no cruelty that hurts me like such cruelty to old age."

Just then another nun came into the room, said something to Sister Denisa in a low voice, and glided out like a silent shadow, her rosary sway· ing back and forth with every movement of her clinging black skirts. "I am needed up-stairs," said Sister Denisa, turning to Joyce. "Will you come up and see the sleeping-rooms?"

They went up the freshly scrubbed steps to a great dormitory, where, against the bare walls, stood long rows of narrow cots. They were all empty, except one at the farthest end, where an old woman lay with her handkerchief across her eyes.

"Poor old Number Thirty-one!" said Sister Denisa. "She seems to feel her unhappy position more than any one in the house. The most of them are thankful for mere bodily comfort, — satisfied with food and shelter and warmth ; but she is continually pining for her old home surroundings. Will you not come and speak to her in English ? She married a countryman of yours, and lived over thirty years in America. She speaks of that time as the happiest in her life. I am sure that you can give her a great deal of pleasure."

"Is she ill?" said Joyce, timidly drawing back as the nun started across the room.

"No, I think not," was the answer. "She says she can't bear to be herded in one room with all those poor creatures, like a flock of sheep, with nothing to do but wait for death. She has always been accustomed to having a room of her own, so that her greatest trial is in having no privacy. She must eat, sleep, and live with a hundred other old women always around her. She comes up here to bed whenever she can find the slightest ache for an excuse, just to be by herself. I wish that we could give her a little spot that she could call her own, and shut the door on, and feel alone. But it cannot be," she added, with a sigh. " It taxes our strength to the utmost to give them all even a bare home."

By this time they had reached the cot, over the head of which hung a card, bearing the number " Thirty-one."

" Here is a little friend to see you, grandmother," said Sister Denisa, placing a chair by the bedside, and stooping to smooth back the locks of silvery hair that had strayed out from under the coarse white night-cap. Then she passed quickly on to her other duties, leaving Joyce to begin the conversation as best she could. The old woman looked at her sharply with piercing dark eyes, which must have been beautiful in their youth. The intense gaze embarrassed Joyce, and to break the silence she hurriedly stammered out the first thing that came to her mind.

"Are you ill, to-day?"

The simple question had a startling effect on the old woman. She raised herself on one

elbow, and reached out for Joyce's hand, drawing her eagerly nearer. "Ah," she cried, "you speak the language that my husband taught me to love, and the tongue my little children lisped ; but they are all dead now, and I've come back to my native land to find no home but the one that charity provides."

Her words ended in a wail, and she sank back on her pillow. "And this is my birth-day," she went on. "Seventy-three years old, and a pauper, cast out to the care of strangers."

The tears ran down her wrinkled cheeks, and her mouth trembled pitifully. Joyce was dis-tressed ; she looked around for Sister Denisa, but saw that they were alone, they two, in the great bare dormitory, with its long rows of narrow white cots. The child felt utterly help-less to speak a word of comfort, although she was so sorry for the poor lonely old creature that she began to cry softly to herself. She leaned over, and taking one of the thin, blue-veined hands in hers, patted it tenderly with her plump little fingers.

"I ought not to complain," said the tremb-ling voice, still broken by sobs. "We have food and shelter and sunshine and the sisters. Ah, that little Sister Denisa, she is indeed a smile of God to us all. But at seventy-three one wants more than a cup of coffee and a clean handkerchief.   One wants something besides a bed and being just Number Thirty-one among two hundred other paupers."

"I am *so* sorry!" exclaimed Joyce, with such heartfelt earnestness that the sobbing woman felt the warmth of her sympathy, and looked up with a brighter face.

"Talk to me," she exclaimed.   "It has been so long since I have heard your language."

While she obeyed Joyce kept thinking of her Grandmother Ware.   She could see her out, doors among her flowers, the dahlias and touch-me-nots, the four-o'clocks and the cinnamon roses, taking such pride and pleasure in her sweet posy beds.   She could see her beside the little table on the shady porch, making tea for some old neighbor who had dropped in to spend the afternoon with her.   Or she was asleep in her armchair by the western window, her Bible in her lap and a smile on her sweet, kindly face.   How dreary and empty the days must seem to poor old Number Thirty-one, with none of these things to brighten them.

Joyce could scarcely keep the tears out of her voice while she talked.   Later, when Sister

Denisa came back, Joyce was softly humming a lullaby, and Number Thirty-one, with a smile on her pitiful old face, was sleeping like a little child.

"You will come again, dear mademoiselle," said Sister Denisa, as she kissed the child good-by at the door. "You have brought a blessing, may you carry one away as well!"

Joyce looked inquiringly at madame. "You may come whenever you like," was the answer. "Marie can bring you whenever you are in town."

Joyce was so quiet on the way home that madame feared the day had been too fatiguing for her. "No," said Joyce, soberly. "I was only thinking about poor old Number Thirty-one. I am sorrier for her than I was for Jules. I used to think that there was nothing so sad as being a little child without any father or mother, and having to live in an asylum. I've often thought how lovely it would be to go around and find a beautiful home for every little orphan in the world. But I believe, now, that it is worse to be old that way. Old people can't play together, and they haven't anything to look forward to, and it makes them so

miserable to remember all the things they have
had and lost. If I had enough money to adopt
anybody, I would adopt some poor old grandfather or grandmother and make'm happy all
the rest of their days."

CHAPTER VIII.

CHRISTMAS PLANS AND AN ACCIDENT.

THAT night, when Marie came in to light the lamps and brush Joyce's hair before dinner, she had some news to tell.

"Brossard has been sent away from the Ciseaux place," she said. "A new man is coming to-morrow, and my friend, Clotilde Robard, has already taken the position of housekeeper. She says that a very different life has begun for little Monsieur Jules, and that in his fine new clothes one could never recognize the little goatherd. He looks now like what he is, a gentleman's son. He has the room next to monsieur's, all freshly furnished, and after New Year a tutor is coming from Paris.

"But they say that it is pitiful to see how greatly the child fears his uncle. He does not understand the old man's cold, forbidding manner, and it provokes monsieur to have the little one tremble and grow pale whenever he speaks. Clotilde says that Madame Gréville told monsieur that the boy needed games and young companions to make him more like other children, and he promised her that Monsieur Jules should come over here to-morrow afternoon to play with you."

"Oh, good!" cried Joyce. "We'll have another barbecue if the day is fine. I am so glad that we do not have to be bothered any more by those tiresome old goats."

By the time the next afternoon arrived, however, Joyce was far too much interested in something else to think of a barbecue. Cousin Kate had come back from Paris with a trunk full of pretty things, and a plan for the coming Christmas. At first she thought of taking only madame into her confidence, and preparing a small Christmas tree for Joyce; but afterwards she concluded that it would give the child more pleasure if she were allowed to take part in the preparations. It would keep her from being homesick by giving her something else to think about.

Then madame proposed inviting a few of the little peasant children who had never seen

a Christmas tree. The more they discussed
the plan the larger it grew, like a rolling
snowball. By lunch-time madame had a list
of thirty children, who were to
be bidden to the Noël fête, and
Cousin Kate had decided to order
a tree tall enough to touch the
ceiling.

When Jules came over, awkward
and shy with the consciousness of
his new clothes, he found Joyce
sitting in the midst of yards of
gaily colored tarletan. It was
heaped up around her in bright
masses of purple and orange
and scarlet and green, and she
was making it into candy-bags
for the tree.

In a few minutes Jules had
forgotten all about himself, and
was as busy as she, pinning the
little stocking-shaped patterns
in place, and carefully cutting out those fascinating bags.

"You would be lots of help," said Joyce, "if
you could come over every day, for there's all

the ornaments to unpack, and the corn to shell, and pop, and string. It will take most of my time to dress the dolls, and there's such a short time to do everything in."

"You never saw any pop-corn, did you, Jules?" asked Cousin Kate. "When I was here last time, I couldn't find it anywhere in France; but the other day a friend told me of a grocer in Paris, who imports it for his American customers every winter. So I went there. Joyce, suppose you get the popper and show Jules what the corn is like."

Madame was interested also, as she watched the little brown kernels shaken back and forth in their wire cage over the glowing coals. When they began popping open, the little seeds suddenly turning into big white blossoms, she sent Rosalie running to bring monsieur to see the novel sight.

"We can eat and work at the same time," said Joyce, as she filled a dish with the corn, and called Jules back to the table, where he had been cutting tarletan. "There's no time to lose. See what a funny grain this is!" she cried, picking up one that lay on the top of the dish. "It looks like Therese, the fishwoman, in her white cap."

"And here is a goat's head," said Jules, picking up another grain. "And this one looks like a fat pigeon."

He had forgotten his shyness entirely now, and was laughing and talking as easily as Jack could have done.

"Jules," said Joyce, suddenly, looking around to see that the older people were too busy with their own conversation to notice hers. "Jules, why don't you talk to your Uncle Martin the way you do to me? He would like you lots better if you would. Robard says that you get pale and frightened every time he speaks to you, and it provokes him for you to be so timid."

Jules dropped his eyes. "I cannot help it," he exclaimed. "He looks so grim and cross that my voice just won't come out of my throat when I open my mouth."

Joyce studied him critically, with her head tipped a little to one side. "Well, I must say," she exclaimed, finally, "that, for a boy born in America, you have the least dare about you of anybody I ever saw. Your Uncle Mar-

tin isn't any grimmer or crosser than a man I
know at home. There's Judge Ward, so big
and solemn and dignified that everybody is
half way afraid of him. Even grown people
have always been particular about what they
said to him.

" Last summer his little nephew, Charley
Ward, came to visit him. Charley's just a
little thing, still in dresses, and he calls his
uncle, Bill. Think of anybody daring to call
Judge Ward, *Bill!* No matter what the judge
was doing, or how glum he looked, if Charley
took a notion, he would go up and stand in
front of him, and say, ' Laugh, Bill, laugh ! ' If
the judge happened to be reading, he'd have to
put down his book, and no matter whether he
felt funny or not, or whether there was anything to laugh at or not, he would have to
throw his head back and just roar. Charley
liked to see his fat sides shake, and his white
teeth shine. I've heard people say that the
judge likes Charley better than anybody else
in the world, because he's the only person who
acts as if he wasn't afraid of him."

Jules sat still a minute, considering, and then
asked, anxiously, " But what do you suppose

would happen if I should say ' Laugh, Martin, laugh,' to my uncle?"

Joyce shrugged her shoulders impatiently. " Mercy, Jules, I did not mean that you should act like a three-year-old baby. I meant that you ought to talk up to your uncle some. Now this is the way you are." She picked up a kernel of the unpopped corn, and held it out for him to see. " You shut yourself up in a little hard ball like this, so that your uncle can't get acquainted with you. How can he know what is inside of your head if you always shut up like a clam whenever he comes near you? This is the way that you ought to be." She shot one of the great white grains towards him with a deft flip of her thumb and finger. " Be free and open with him."

Jules put the tender morsel in his mouth and ate it thoughtfully. " I'll try," he promised, " if you really think that it would please him, and I can think of anything to say. You don't know how I dread going to the table when everything is always so still that we can hear the clock tick."

" Well, you take my advice," said Joyce. " Talk about anything. Tell him about our

Thanksgiving feast and the Christmas tree, and ask him if you can't come over every day to help. I wouldn't let anybody think that I was a coward."

Joyce's little lecture had a good effect, and monsieur saw the wisdom of Madame Gréville's advice when Jules came to the table that night. He had brought a handful of the wonderful corn to show his uncle, and in the conversation that it brought about he unconsciously showed something else, — something of his sensitive inner self that aroused his uncle's interest.

Every afternoon of the week that followed found Jules hurrying over to Madame Gréville's to help with the Christmas preparations. He strung yards of corn, and measured out the nuts and candy for each of the gay bags. Twice he went in the carriage to Tours with Cousin Kate and Joyce, to help buy presents for the thirty little guests. He was jostled by the holiday shoppers in crowded aisles. He stood enraptured in front of wonderful show windows, and he had the joy of choosing fifteen things from piles of bright tin trumpets, drums, jumping-jacks, and picture-books. Joyce chose the presents for the girls,

The tree was bought and set up in a large unused room back of the library, and as soon as each article was in readiness it was carried in and laid on a table beside it. Jules used to steal in sometimes and look at the tapers, the beautiful colored glass balls, the gilt stars and glittering tinsel, and wonder how the stately cedar would look in all that array of loveliness. Everything belonging to it seemed sacred, even the unused scraps of bright tarletan and the bits of broken candles. He would not let Marie sweep them up to be burned, but gathered them carefully into a box and carried them home. There were several things that he had rescued from her broom, — one of those beautiful red balls, cracked on one side it is true, but gleaming like a mammoth red cherry on the other. There were scraps of tinsel and odds and ends of ornaments that had been broken or damaged by careless handling. These he hid away in a chest in his room, as carefully as a miser would have hoarded a bag of gold.

Clotilde Robard, the housekeeper, wondered why she found his candle burned so low several mornings. She would have wondered still more if she had gone into his room a while before daybreak. He had awakened early, and, sitting up in bed with the quilts wrapped around him, spread the scraps of tarletan on his knees. He was piecing together with his awkward little fingers enough to make several tiny bags.

Henri missed his spade one morning, and hunted for it until he was out of patience. It was nowhere to be seen. Half an hour later, coming back to the house, he found it hanging in its usual place, where he had looked for it a dozen times at least. Jules had taken it down to the woods to dig up a little cedar-tree, so little that it was not over a foot high when it was planted in a box.

Clotilde had to be taken into the secret, for he could not hide it from her. " It is for my Uncle Martin," he said, timidly. " Do you think he will like it ? "

The motherly housekeeper looked at the poor little tree, decked out in its scraps of cast-off finery, and felt a sob rising in her throat, but she held up her hands with many admiring exclamations that made Jules glow with pride.

"SITTING UP IN BED WITH THE QUILTS WRAPPED
AROUND HIM,"

"I have no beautiful white strings of pop-corn to hang over it like wreaths of snow," he said, "so I am going down the lane for some mistletoe that grows in one of the highest trees. The berries are like lovely white wax beads."

"You are a good little lad," said the house-keeper, kindly, as she gave his head an affec-tionate pat. "I shall have to make something to hang on that tree myself; some gingerbread figures, maybe. I used to know how to cut out men and horses and pigs, — nearly all the animals. I must try it again some day soon."

A happy smile spread all over Jules's face as he thanked her. The words, "You are a good little lad," sent a warm glow of pleasure through him, and rang like music in his ears all the way down the lane. How bright the world looked this frosty December morning! What cheeri-ness there was in the ring of Henri's axe as he chopped away at the stove-wood! What friend-liness in the baker's whistle, as he rattled by in his big cart! Jules found himself whistling, too, for sheer gladness, and all because of no more kindness than might have been thrown to a dog ; a pat on the head and the words, "You are a good little lad."

Sometime after, it may have been two hours or more, Madame Gréville was startled by a wild, continuous ringing of the bell at her front gate. Somebody was sending peal after peal echoing through the garden, with quick, impatient jerks of the bell-wire. She hurried out herself to answer the summons.

Berthé had already shot back the bolt and showed Clotilde leaning against the stone post, holding her fat sides and completely exhausted by her short run from the Ciseaux house.

"Will madame send Gabriel for the doctor?" she cried, gasping for breath at every word. "The little Monsieur Jules has fallen from a tree and is badly hurt. We do not know how much, for he is still unconscious and his uncle is away from home. Henri found him lying under a tree with a big bunch of mistletoe in his arms. He carried him up-stairs while I ran over to ask you to send Gabriel quickly on a horse for the doctor."

"Gabriel shall go immediately," said Madame

Gréville, "and I shall follow you as soon as I have given the order."

Clotilde started back in as great haste as her weight would allow, puffing and blowing and wiping her eyes on her apron at every step. Madame overtook her before she had gone many rods. Always calm and self-possessed in every emergency, madame took command now; sent the weeping Clotilde to look for old linen, Henri to the village for Monsieur Ciseaux, and then turned her attention to Jules.

"To think," said Clotilde, coming into the room, "that the last thing the poor little lamb did was to show me his Christmas tree that he was making ready for his uncle!" She pointed to the corner where it stood, decked by awkward boyish hands in its pitiful collection of scraps.

"Poor little fellow!" said madame, with tears in her own eyes. "He has done the best he could. Put it in the closet, Clotilde. Jules would not want it to be seen before Christmas."

Madame stayed until the doctor had made his visit; then the report that she carried home was that Jules had regained consciousness, and that, as far as could be discovered, his only injury was a broken leg.

Joyce took refuge in the pear-tree. It was not alone because Jules was hurt that she wanted to cry, but because they must have the Noël fête without him. She knew how bitterly he would be disappointed.

CHAPTER IX.

A GREAT DISCOVERY.

"ONLY two more nights till Christmas eve, two more nights, two more nights," sang Joyce to Jules in a sort of chant. She was sitting beside his bed with a box in her lap, full of little dolls, which she was dressing. Every day since his accident she had been allowed to make him two visits, — one in the morning, and one in the afternoon. They helped wonderfully in shortening the long, tedious days for Jules. True, Madame Gréville came often with broths and jellies, Cousin Kate made flying visits to leave rare hothouse grapes and big bunches of violets; Clotilde hung over him with motherly tenderness, and his uncle looked into the room many times a day to see that he wanted nothing.

Jules's famished little heart drank in all this unusual kindness and attention as greedily as the parched earth drinks in the rain. Still, he would have passed many a long, restless hour, had it not been for Joyce's visits.

She brought over a photograph of the house at home, with the family seated in a group on the front porch. Jules held it close while she introduced each one of them. By the time he had heard all about Holland's getting lost the day the circus came to town, and Jack's taking the prize in a skating contest, and Mary's set-ting her apron on fire, and the baby's sweet little ways when he said his prayers, or played peek-a-boo, he felt very well acquainted with the entire Ware family. Afterward, when Joyce had gone, he felt his loneliness more than ever. He lay there, trying to imagine how it must feel to have a mother and sisters and brothers all as fond of each other as Joyce's were, and to live in the midst of such good times as always went on in the little brown house.

Monsieur Ciseaux, sitting by his fire with the door open between the two rooms, listened to Joyce's merry chatter with almost as much interest as Jules. He would have been ashamed to admit how eagerly he listened for her step on

the stairs every day, or what longings wakened
in his lonely old heart, when he sat by his loveless fireside after she had gone home, and there
was no more sound of children's voices in the
next room.

There had been good times in the old
Ciseaux house also, once, and two little
brothers and a sister had played in that very
room ; but they had grown up long ago, and
the ogre of selfishness and misunderstanding
had stolen in and killed all their happiness.
Ah, well, there was much that the world
would never know about that misunderstanding. There was much to forgive and forget
on both sides.

Joyce had a different story for each visit.
To-day she had just finished telling Jules the
fairy tale of which he never tired, the tale of
the giant scissors.

" I never look at those scissors over the
gate without thinking of you," said Jules,
"and the night when you played that I was
the Prince, and you came to rescue me."

" I wish I could play scissors again, and
rescue somebody else that I know," answered
Joyce. " I'd take poor old Number Thirty-one

away from the home of the Little Sisters of the Poor."

" What's Number Thirty-one? " asked Jules. " You never told me about that."

" Didn't I ? " asked Joyce, in surprise. " She is a lonely old woman that the sisters take care of. I have talked about her so often, and written home so much, that I thought I had told everybody. I can hardly keep from crying whenever I think of her. Marie and I stop every day we go into town and take her flowers. I have been there four times since my first visit with madame. Sometimes she tells me things that happened when she was a little girl here in France, but she talks to me oftenest in English about the time when she lived in America. I can hardly imagine that she was ever as young as I am, and that she romped with her brothers as I did with Jack."

" Tell some of the things that she told you," urged Jules ; so Joyce began repeating all that she knew about Number Thirty-one.

It was a pathetic little tale that brought tears to Jules's eyes, and a dull pain to the heart of the old man who listened in the next room. "I wish I were rich," exclaimed

Joyce, impulsively, as she finished. " I wish I had a beautiful big home, and I would adopt her for my grandmother. She should have a great lovely room, where the sun shines in all day long, and it should be furnished in rose-color like the one that she had when she was a girl. I'd dress her in gray satin and soft white lace. She has the prettiest silvery hair, and beautiful dark eyes. She would make a lovely grandmother. And I would have a maid to wait on her, and there'd be mignonette always growing in boxes on the window-sill. Every time I came back from town, I'd bring her a present just for a nice little surprise ; and I'd read to her, and sing to her, and make her feel that she belonged to somebody, so that she'd be happy all the rest of her days.

" Yesterday while I was there she was holding a little cut glass vinaigrette. It had a big D engraved on the silver top. She said that it was the only thing that she had left except her wedding ring, and that it was to be Sister Denisa's when she was gone. The D stands for both their names. Hers is Désiré. She said the vinaigrette was too precious to part with as long as she lives, because her oldest brother gave it to her on her twelfth birthday, when she was exactly as old as I am. Isn't Désiré a pretty name?"

"Mademoiselle," called Monsieur Ciseaux from the next room, "mademoiselle, will you come — will you tell me — what name was that? Désiré, did you say?"

There was something so strange in the way he called that name Désiré, almost like a cry, that Joyce sprang up, startled, and ran into the next room. She had never ventured inside before.

"Tell me again what you were telling Jules," said the old man. "Seventy-three years, did you say? And how long has she been back in France?"

Joyce began to answer his rapid questions, but stopped with a frightened cry as her glance fell on a large portrait hanging over the mantel. "There she is!" she cried, excitedly dancing up and down as she pointed to the portrait. "There she is! That's Number Thirty-one, her very own self."

"You are mistaken!" cried the old man, attempting to rise from his chair, but trembling so that he could scarcely pull himself up on his

"'THAT'S NUMBER THIRTY-ONE.'"

feet. "That is a picture of my mother, and Désiré is dead; long dead."

"But it is *exactly* like Number Thirty-one, — I mean Madame Désiré," persisted Joyce.

Monsieur looked at her wildly from under his shaggy brows, and then, turning away, began to pace up and down the room. "I had a sister once," he began. "She would have been seventy-three this month, and her name was Désiré."

Joyce stood motionless in the middle of the room, wondering what was coming next. Suddenly turning with a violence that made her start, he cried, "No, I never can forgive! She has been dead to me nearly a lifetime. Why did you tell me this, child? Out of my sight! What is it to me if she is homeless and alone? Go! Go!"

He waved his hands so wildly in motioning her away, that Joyce ran out of the room and banged the door behind her.

"What do you suppose is the matter with him?" asked Jules, in a frightened whisper, as they listened to his heavy tread, back and forth, back and forth, in the next room.

Joyce shook her head. "I don't know for

sure," she answered, hesitatingly, "but I be
lieve that he is going crazy."

Jules's eyes opened so wide that Joyce wished
she had not frightened him. "Oh, you know
that I didn't mean it," she said, reassuringly.
The heavy tread stopped, and the children
looked at each other.

"What can he be doing now?" Jules asked,
anxiously.

Joyce tiptoed across the room, and peeped
through the keyhole. "He is sitting down
now, by the table, with his head on his arms.
He looks as if he might be crying about something."

"I wish he didn't feel bad," said Jules, with
a swift rush of pity. "He has been so good
to me ever since he sent Brossard away. Sometimes I think that he must feel as much alone
in the world as I do, because all his family are
dead, too. Before I broke my leg I was making
him a little Christmas tree, so that he need not
feel left out when we had the big one. I was
getting mistletoe for it when I fell. I can't
finish it now, but there's five pieces of candle on
it, and I'll get Clotilde to light them while the
fête is going on, so that I'll not miss the big

tree so much. Oh, nobody knows how much I want to go to that fête! Sometimes it seems more than I can bear to have to stay away."

"Where is your tree?" asked Joyce. "May I see it?"

Jules pointed to the closet. "It's in there," he said, proudly. "I trimmed it with pieces that Marie swept up to burn. Oh, shut the door! Quick!" he cried, excitedly, as a step was heard in the hall. "I don't want anybody to see it before the time comes."

The step was Henri's. He had come to say that Marie was waiting to take mademoiselle home. Joyce was glad of the interruption. She could not say anything in praise of the poor little tree, and she knew that Jules expected her to. She felt relieved that Henri's presence made it impossible for her to express any opinion.

She bade Jules good-by gaily, but went home with such a sober little face that Cousin Kate began to question her about her visit. Madame, sitting by the window with her embroidery-frame, heard the account also. Several times she looked significantly across at Cousin Kate, over the child's head.

"Joyce," said Cousin Kate, "you have had so little outdoor exercise since Jules's accident that it would be a good thing for you to run around in the garden awhile before dark."

Joyce had not seen madame's glances, but she felt vaguely that Cousin Kate was making an excuse to get rid of her. She was disappointed, for she thought that her account of monsieur's queer actions and Jules's little tree would have made a greater impression on her audience. She went out obediently, walking up and down the paths with her hands in her jacket pockets, and her red tam-o'shanter pulled down over her eyes. The big white cat followed her, ran on ahead, and then stopped, arching its back as if waiting for her to stroke it. Taking no notice of it, Joyce turned aside to the pear-tree and climbed up among the highest branches.

The cat rubbed against the tree, mewing and purring by turns, then sprang up in the tree after her. She took the warm, furry creature in her arms and began talking to it.

"Oh, Solomon," she said, "what do you suppose is the matter over there? My poor old lady must be monsieur's sister, or she couldn't have looked exactly like that picture, and he would not have acted so queerly. What do you suppose it is that he can never forgive? Why did he call me in there and then drive me out in such a crazy way, and tramp around the room, and put his head down on his arms as if he were crying?"

Solomon purred louder and closed his eyes.

"Oh, you dear, comfortable old thing," exclaimed Joyce, giving the cat a shake. "Wake up and take some interest in what I am saying. I wish you were as smart as Puss in Boots; then maybe you could find out what is the matter. How I wish fairy tales could be true! I'd say 'Giant scissors, right the wrong and open the gate that's been shut so long.' There! Did you hear that, Solomon Gréville? I said a rhyme right off without waiting to make it up. Then the scissors would leap down and cut the misunderstanding or trouble or whatever it is, and the gate would fly open, and there the brother and sister would meet each other. All the unhappy years would be forgotten, and they'd take each other by the hand, just as they did when they were little children, Martin and Désiré, and go into the old home together, — on Christmas Day, in the morning."

Joyce was half singing her words now, as she rocked the cat back and forth in her arms. " And then the scissors would bring Jules a magnificent big tree, and he'd never be afraid of his uncle any more. Oh, they'd all have such a happy time on Christmas Day, in the morning ! "

Joyce had fully expected to be homesick all during the holidays ; but now she was so absorbed in other people's troubles, and her day-dreams to make everybody happy, that she forgot all about herself. She fairly bubbled over with the peace and good-will of the approaching Christmas-tide, and rocked the cat back and forth in the pear-tree to the tune of a happy old-time carol.

A star or two twinkled out through the

gloaming, and, looking up beyond them through the infinite stretches of space, Joyce thought of a verse that she and Jack had once learned together, one rainy Sunday at her Grandmother Ware's, sitting on a little stool at the old lady's feet :

"Behold thou hast made the heaven and the earth by thy great power and outstretched arm, and *there is nothing too hard for thee."* Her heart gave a bound at the thought. Why should she be sitting there longing for fairy tales to be true, when the great Hand that had set the stars to swinging could bring anything to pass ; could even open that long-closed gate and bring the brother and sister together again, and send happiness to little Jules ?

Joyce lifted her eyes again and looked up, out past the stars. "Oh, if you please, God," she whispered, "for the little Christ-child's sake."

When Joyce went back to the house, Cousin Kate sat in the drawing-room alone. Madame had gone over to see Jules, and did not return until long after dark. Berthé had been in three times to ask monsieur if dinner should be served, before they heard her ring at the gate. When she finally came, there was such an air of mystery about her that Joyce was puzzled. All that next morning, too, the day before Christmas, it seemed to Joyce as if something unusual were afloat. Everybody in the house was acting strangely.

Madame and Cousin Kate did not come home to lunch. She had been told that she must not go to see Jules until afternoon, and the doors of the room where the Christmas tree was kept had all been carefully locked. She thought that the morning never would pass. It was nearly three o'clock when she started over to see Jules. To her great surprise, as she ran lightly up the stairs to his room, she saw her Cousin Kate hurrying across the upper hall, with a pile of rose-colored silk curtains in her arms.

Jules tried to raise himself up in bed as Joyce entered, forgetting all about his broken leg in his eagerness to tell the news. "Oh, what do you think!" he cried. "They said that I might be the one to tell you. She *is* Uncle Martin's sister, the old woman you told about yesterday, and he is going to bring her home to-morrow."

Joyce sank into a chair with a little gasp at the suddenness of his news. She had not expected this beautiful ending of her day-dreams to be brought about so soon, although she had hoped that it would be sometime.

"How did it all happen?" she cried, with a beaming face. "Tell me about it! Quick!"

"Yesterday afternoon madame came over soon after you left. She gave me my wine jelly, and then went into Uncle Martin's room, and talked and talked for the longest time. After she had gone he did not eat any dinner, and I think that he must have sat up all night, for I heard him walking around every time that I waked up. Very early this morning, madame came back again, and M. Gréville was with her. They drove with Uncle Martin to the Little Sisters of the Poor. I don't know what happened out there, only that Aunt Désiré is to be brought home to-morrow.

"Your Cousin Kate was with them when they came back, and they had brought all sorts of things with them from Tours. She is in there now, making Aunt Désiré's room look like it did when she was a girl."

"Oh, isn't it lovely!" exclaimed Joyce. "It

is better than all the fairy tales that I have ever read or heard, — almost too good to be true!" Just then Cousin Kate called her, and she ran across the hall. Standing in the doorway, she looked all around the freshly furnished room, that glowed with the same soft, warm pink that colors the heart of a shell.

"How beautiful!" cried Joyce, glancing from the rose on the dressing-table to the soft curtains of the windows, which all opened towards the morning sun. "What a change it will be from that big bare dormitory with its rows of narrow little cots." She tiptoed around the room, admiring everything, and smiling over the happiness in store for poor old Number Thirty-one, when she should find herself in the midst of such loveliness.

Joyce's cup of pleasure was so full, that it brimmed over when they turned to leave the room. Cousin Kate slipped an arm around her, and kissed her softly on the forehead.

"You dear little fairy tale lover," she said. "Do you know that it is because of you that this desert has blossomed? If you had never made all those visits to the Little Sisters of the Poor, and had never won old Madame Désiré's love and confidence by your sympathy, if you had never told Jules the story of the giant scissors, and wished so loud that you could fly to her rescue, old monsieur would never have known that his sister is living. Even then, I doubt if he would have taken this step, and brought her back home to live, if your stories of your mother and the children had not brought his own childhood back to him. He said that he used to sit there hour after hour, and hear you talk of your life at home, until some of its warmth and love crept into his own frozen old heart, and thawed out its selfishness and pride."

Joyce lifted her radiant face, and looked towards the half opened window, as she caught the sound of chimes. Across the Loire came the deep-toned voice of a cathedral bell, ringing for vespers.

"Listen!" she cried. "Peace on earth, — good-will — oh, Cousin Kate! It really does seem to say it! My Christmas has begun the day before."

CHAPTER X.

CHRISTMAS.

LONG before the Christmas dawn was bright enough to bring the blue parrots into plain view on the walls of Joyce's room, she had climbed out of bed to look for her "messages from Noël." The night before, following the old French custom, she had set her little slippers just outside the threshold. Now, candle in hand, she softly slipped to the door and peeped out into the hall. Her first eager glance showed that they were full.

Climbing back into her warm bed, she put the candle on the table beside it, and began emptying the slippers. They were filled with bonbons and all sorts of little trifles, such as she and Jules had admired in the gay shop windows. On the top of one madame had laid a slender silver pencil, and monsieur a pretty purse. In the other was a pair of little wooden shoes, fashioned like the ones that Jules had worn when she first knew him. They were only half as long as her thumb, and wrapped in a paper on which was written that Jules himself had whittled them out for her, with Henri's help and instructions.

"What little darlings!" exclaimed Joyce. "I hope he will think as much of the scrapbook that I made for him as I do of these. I know that he will be pleased with the big microscope that Cousin Kate bought for him."

She spread all the things out on the table, and gave the slippers a final shake. A red morocco case, no larger than half a dollar, fell out of the toe of one of them. Inside the case was a tiny buttonhole watch, with its wee hands pointing to six o'clock. It was the smallest watch that Joyce had ever seen, Cousin Kate's gift. Joyce could hardly keep back a little squeal of delight. She wanted to wake up everybody on the place and show it. Then she wished that she could be back in the brown house, showing it to her mother and the children. For a moment, as she thought of them, sharing the pleasure of their Christmas stockings without her, a great wave of homesickness swept over her, and she lay back on the pillow with that miserable, far-away feeling that, of all things, makes one most desolate.

Then she heard the rapid "tick, tick, tick, tick," of the little watch, and was comforted. She had not realized before that time could go so fast. Now thirty seconds were gone; then sixty. At this rate it could not be such a very long time before they would be packing their trunks to start home; so Joyce concluded not to make herself unhappy by longing for the family, but to get as much pleasure as possible out of this strange Christmas abroad.

That little watch seemed to make the morning fly. She looked at it at least twenty times an hour. She had shown it to every one in the house, and was wishing that she could take it over to Jules for him to see, when Monsieur Ciseaux's carriage stopped at the gate. He was on his way to the Little Sisters of the Poor, and had come to ask Joyce to drive with him to bring his sister home.

He handed her into the carriage as if she had been a duchess, and then seemed to forget that she was beside him; for nothing was said all the way. As the horses spun along the road in the keen morning air, the old man was

busy with his memories, his head dropped forward on his breast. The child watched him,
entering into this little drama as sympatheti-
cally as if she herself were the forlorn old
woman, and this silent, white-haired man at
her side were Jack.

Sister Denisa came running out to meet
them, her face shining and her eyes glisten-
ing with tears. "It is for joy that I weep,"
she exclaimed, "that poor madame should have
come to her own again. See the change that
has already been made in her by the blessed
news."

Joyce looked down the corridor as monsieur
hurried forward to meet the old lady coming
towards them, and to offer his arm. Hope had
straightened the bowed figure; joy had put
lustre into her dark eyes and strength into her
weak frame. She walked with such proud
stateliness that the other inmates of the home
looked up at her in surprise as she passed.
She was no more like the tearful, broken-
spirited woman who had lived among them so
long, than her threadbare dress was like the
elegant mantle which monsieur had brought to
fold around her.

Joyce had brought a handful of roses to Sister Denisa, who caught them up with a cry of pleasure, and held them against her face as if they carried with them some sweetness of another world.

Madame came up then, and, taking the nun in her arms, tried to thank her for all that she had done, but could find no words for a gratitude so deep, and turned away, sobbing.

They said good-by to Sister Denisa, — brave Little Sister of the Poor, whose only joy was the pleasure of unselfish service ; who had no time to even stand at the gate and be a glad witness of other people's Christmas happiness, but must hurry back to her morning task of dealing out coffee and clean handkerchiefs to two hundred old paupers. No, there were only a hundred and ninety-nine now. Down the streets, across the Loire, into the old village and out again, along the wide Paris road, one of them was going home.

The carriage turned and went for a little space between brown fields and closely clipped hedgerows, and then madame saw the windows of her old home flashing back the morning sunlight over the high stone wall. Again the carriage turned, into the lane this time, and now the sunlight was caught up by the scissors over the gate, and thrown dazzlingly down into their faces.

Monsieur smiled as he looked at Joyce, a tender, gentle smile that one would have supposed never could have been seen on those harsh lips. She was almost standing up in the carriage, in her excitement.

"Oh, it has come true!" she cried, clasping her hands together. "The gates are really opening at last!"

Yes, the Ogre, whatever may have been its name, no longer lived. Its spell was broken, for now the giant scissors no longer barred the way. Slowly the great gate swung open, and the carriage passed through. Joyce sprang out and ran on ahead to open the door. Hand in hand, just as when they were little children, Martin and Désiré, this white-haired brother and sister went back to the old home together ; and it was Christmas Day, in the morning.

At five o'clock that evening the sound of Gabriel's accordeon went echoing up and down the garden, and thirty little children

were marching to its music along the paths, between the rows of blooming laurel. Joyce understood, now, why the room where the Christmas tree stood had been kept so carefully locked. For two days that room had been empty and the tree had been standing in Monsieur Ciseaux's parlor. Cousin Kate and madame and Berthé and Marie and Gabriel had all been over there, busily at work, and neither she nor Jules had suspected what was going on down-stairs.

Now she marched with the others, out of the garden and across the road, keeping time to the music of the wheezy old accordeon that Gabriel played so proudly. Surely every soul, in all that long procession filing through the gate of the giant scissors, belonged to the

kingdom of loving hearts and gentle hands;
for they were all children who passed through,
or else mothers who carried in their arms the
little ones who, but for these faithful arms,
must have missed this Noël fête.

Jules had been carried down-stairs and laid
on a couch in the corner of the room where he
could see the tree to its best advantage. Beside
him sat his great-aunt, Désiré, dressed in a
satin gown of silvery gray that had been her
mother's, and looking as if she had just stepped
out from the frame of the portrait up-stairs.
She held Jules's hand in hers, as if with it she
grasped the other Jules, the little brother of
the olden days for whom this child had been
named. And she told him stories of his grandfather and his father. Then Jules found that

this Aunt Désiré had known his mother; had once sat on the vine-covered porch while he ran after fireflies on the lawn in his little white dress; had heard the song the voice still sang to him in his dreams:

" Till the stars and the angels come to keep
    Their watch where my baby lies fast asleep."

When she told him this, with her hand stroking his and folding it tight with many tender little claspings, he felt that he had found a part of his old home, too, as well as Aunt Désiré.

One by one the tapers began to glow on the great tree, and when it was all ablaze the doors were opened for the children to flock in. They stood about the room, bewildered at first, for not one of them had ever seen such a sight before; a tree that glittered and sparkled and shone, that bore stars and rainbows and snow wreaths and gay toys. At first they only drew deep, wondering breaths, and looked at each other with shining eyes. It was all so beautiful and so strange.

Joyce flew here and there, helping to distribute the gifts, feeling her heart grow warmer and warmer as she watched the happy children. "My little daughter never had anything like that in all her life," said one grateful mother as Joyce laid a doll in the child's outstretched arms. "She'll never forget this to her dying day, nor will any of us, dear mademoiselle! We knew not what it was to have so beautiful a Noël!"

When the last toy had been stripped from the branches, it was Cousin Kate's turn to be surprised. At a signal from madame, the children began circling around the tree, singing a song that the sisters at the village school had taught them for the occasion. It was a happy little song about the green pine-tree, king of all trees and monarch of the woods, because of the crown he yearly wears at Noël. At the close every child came up to madame and Cousin Kate and Joyce, to say "Thank you, madame," and "Good night," in the politest way possible.

Gabriel's accordeon led them out again, and the music, growing fainter and fainter, died away in the distance; but in every heart that heard it had been born a memory whose music could never be lost,—the memory of one happy Christmas.

Joyce drew a long breath when it was all over, and, with her arm around Madame Désiré's shoulder, smiled down at Jules.

"How beautifully it has all ended!" she exclaimed. "I am sorry that we have come to the place to say 'and they all lived happily ever after,' for that means that it is time to shut the book."

"Dear heart," murmured Madame Désiré, drawing the child closer to her, "it means that a far sweeter story is just beginning, and it is you who have opened the book for me."

Joyce flushed with pleasure, saying, "I thought this Christmas would be so lonely; but it has been the happiest of my life."

"And mine, too," said Monsieur Ciseaux from the other side of Jules's couch. He took the little fellow's hand in his. "They told me about the tree that you prepared for me. I have been up to look at it, and now I have come to thank you." To the surprise of every one in the room, monsieur bent over and kissed the flushed little face on the pillow. Jules reached up, and, putting his arms around his uncle's neck, laid his cheek a moment

"HE TOOK THE LITTLE FELLOW'S HAND IN HIS."

against the face of his stern old kinsman. Not a word was said, but in that silent caress every barrier of coldness and reserve was forever broken down between them. So the little Prince came into his kingdom, — the kingdom of love and real home happiness.

It is summer now, and far away in the little brown house across the seas Joyce thinks of her happy winter in France and the friends that she found through the gate of the giant scissors. And still those scissors hang over the gate, and may be seen to this day, by any one who takes the trouble to walk up the hill from the little village that lies just across the river Loire, from the old town of Tours.

THE END.

Cosy Corner Series

Each 16mo, cloth decorative, per volume . . $0.75

By *CAROLINE E. JACOBS*

BAB'S CHRISTMAS AT STANHOPE
The story of Bab, a little girl, who is obliged to spend Christmas away from home with three maiden great-aunts.

THE CHRISTMAS SURPRISE PARTY
"The book is written with brisk and deft cleverness."
— *New York Sun.*

A CHRISTMAS PROMISE
A tender and appealing little story.

By *CHARLES DICKENS*

A CHRISTMAS CAROL
No introduction is needed to Dickens' masterpiece, which so wonderfully portrays the Christmas spirit.

A CHILD'S DREAM OF A STAR
One of those beautiful, fanciful little allegories which Dickens alone knew how to write.

By *OUIDA (Louise de la Ramée)*

A DOG OF FLANDERS
A Christmas Story.
Too well and favorably known to require description.

THE NURNBERG STOVE
This beautiful story has never before been published at a popular price.

THE LITTLE EARL
"Boy and girl readers will find entertainment in the story, which is cleverly and skilfully written." — *Boston Transcript.*

B—1

By MISS MULOCK

THE LITTLE LAME PRINCE

A delightful story of a little boy who has many adventures by means of the magic gifts of his fairy godmother.

ADVENTURES OF A BROWNIE

The story of a household elf who torments the cook and gardener, but is a constant joy and delight to the children who love and trust him.

HIS LITTLE MOTHER

Miss Mulock's short stories for children are a constant source of delight to them, and " His Little Mother," in this new and attractive dress, will be welcomed by hosts of youthful readers.

LITTLE SUNSHINE'S HOLIDAY

An attractive story of a summer outing. " Little Sunshine " is another of those beautiful child-characters for which Miss Mulock is so justly famous.

By WILL ALLEN DROMGOOLE

THE FARRIER'S DOG AND HIS FELLOW

This story will appeal to all that is best in the natures of the many admirers of her graceful and piquant style.

THE FORTUNES OF THE FELLOW

Those who read and enjoyed " The Farrier's Dog and His Fellow " will welcome the further account of the adventures of Baydaw and the Fellow.

THE BEST OF FRIENDS

This story continues the experiences of the Farrier's dog and his Fellow.

DOWN IN DIXIE

A fascinating story of a family of Alabama children who move to Florida and grow up in the South.

B—2

By EDITH ROBINSON

A LITTLE PURITAN'S FIRST CHRISTMAS

A story of Colonial times in Boston, telling how Christmas was invented by Betty Sewall, a typical child of the Puritans, aided by her brother Sam.

A LITTLE DAUGHTER OF LIBERTY

The author introduces this story as follows:

" One ride is memorable in the early history of the American Revolution, the well-known ride of Paul Revere. Equally deserving of commendation is another ride, — the ride of Anthony Severn, — which was no less historic in its action or memorable in its consequences."

A LOYAL LITTLE MAID

A delightful and interesting story of Revolutionary days, in which the child heroine, Betsey Schuyler, renders important services to George Washington.

A LITTLE PURITAN REBEL

This is an historical tale of a real girl, during the time when the gallant Sir Harry Vane was governor of Massachusetts.

A LITTLE PURITAN PIONEER

The scene of this story is laid in the Puritan settlement at Charlestown.

A LITTLE PURITAN BOUND GIRL

A story of Boston in Puritan days, which is of great interest to youthful readers.

A LITTLE PURITAN CAVALIER

" The charm and historical value of the author's stories of child life in Colonial days have brought them wide popularity."—*The Independent*.

A PURITAN KNIGHT ERRANT

The story tells of a young lad in Colonial times who endeavored to carry out the high ideals of the knights of olden days.

B—3

By CHARLES G. D. ROBERTS

THE CRUISE OF THE YACHT DIDO
 The story of two boys who turned their yacht into a
fishing boat to earn money.

THE YOUNG ACADIAN
 The story of a young lad of Acadia who rescued a little
English girl from the hands of savages.

THE LORD OF THE AIR
 THE STORY OF THE EAGLE.

THE KING OF THE MAMOZEKEL
 THE STORY OF THE MOOSE.

THE WATCHERS OF THE CAMP - FIRE
 THE STORY OF THE PANTHER.

THE HAUNTER OF THE PINE GLOOM
 THE STORY OF THE LYNX.

THE RETURN TO THE TRAILS
 THE STORY OF THE BEAR.

THE LITTLE PEOPLE OF THE SYCAMORE
 THE STORY OF THE RACCOON.

By JULIANA HORATIA EWING

THE STORY OF A SHORT LIFE
 This beautiful and pathetic story will never grow old.
It is a part of the world's literature, and will never die.

JACKANAPES
 A new edition, with new illustrations, of this exquisite
and touching story, dear alike to young and old.

A GREAT EMERGENCY
 A bright little story of a happy, mischievous family
of children.
B—4

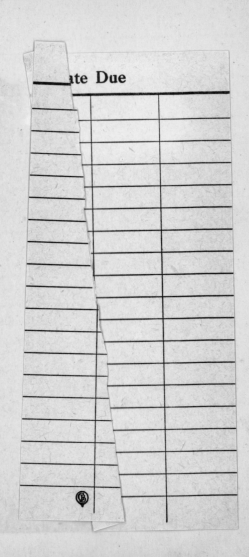

ate Due